Pra

CW00504669

"A great little book that confronts the dark dragons that oppress us in these times"

—**Antonia Arslan**

"a fascinating contemporary St. George, who . . . fights against the devious dragon that today threatens all of us."

—**Archbishop Anoushavan Tanielian**, Prelate of the Eastern Prelacy of the Armenian Apostolic Church of America.

"Siobhan Nash-Marshall has written a . . . beautiful story about a man who discovers, as if by accident, what life is really all about. But there never are just "accidents" in life. There are moments when meaning and truth simply show up and overwhelm us. The result is true peace through the experience of love and the understanding that reality has a meaning that permits us to make sense of our lives."

—**Fr. Gerald E. Murray**, Pastor, Church of the Holy Family, New York, NY

"Siobhan Nash-Marshall reminds me of C. S. Lewis. . . . Like Lewis, she uses old stories to teach timeless truths in a new way. With the eye of the true philosopher, she shows that the distance between what is and what I want can be wider than the abyss that separates heaven from hell. . . . This is storytelling at its most depth-delvingly profound."

—**Joseph Pearce**

"This little book captures what happens to people who live in unreality, they become sub-human and are more like animals. George is a seeker and one who remembers well. He is happiest when he is in the presence of beautiful music or the real love of a good family. These experiences are reality. He has to make choices."

—**Mary Ellen Bork**

GEORGE

GEORGE

Siobhan Nash-Marshall

A Crossroad Book
The Crossroad Publishing Company
New York

The Crossroad Publishing Company
www.CrossroadPublishing.com
© 2022 by Siobhan Nash-Marshall

Cover and text design by Tim Holtz

Library of Congress Cataloging-in-Publication Data available from the Library of Congress.

ISBN 9780824596095 (trade paperback)
ISBN 9780824596101 (EPUB)

Books published by The Crossroad Publishing Company may be purchased at special quantity discount rates for classes and institutional use. For information, please e-mail sales@CrossroadPublishing.com.

Printed in the United States of America

To the Little Ones

an angel of the Lord appeared to Joseph in a
dream. 'Get up!' he said. 'Take the Child and His
mother and flee to Egypt. Stay there until I tell you,
for Herod is going to search for the Child to kill Him.'
(Matthew 2:13)

I

It was not that he didn't love the house. He knew it. He knew the quirky wiring and inlaid floors, the hidden faucets, where the walls had been sheetrocked, where the old air conditioners had once been. There were times when he would stop and breathe in its proportions: the enameled steel doorframes, the open doors, the staircase, the high ceilings. He would gaze at the darker rooms opening behind the doors on the other side of the hall, at the outlines of the books in the tall, tall shelves, at the shape of the carob wood desk on the left, at the long wing of the piano. Something would stir in him when he did, some unknown yet recognized yearning, that same breathtaking yearning that he had felt when they used to drive through those long tunnels on the highway what felt like an eternity ago: the certainty that there was something beyond, and that he was making for it.

He didn't see the cracks in the wall, or the chips in the floor, when he absorbed the house: the bubbled paint on the column in the library, the rust on the storm windows, the stains over the doorway, the hundreds and hundreds of little things that stood out like smudged lipstick on a statue. He saw the house and why he had come to know her secrets: the love of her builders, their hidden aspirations, their joy. He knew why he could spend hours and hours sanding and puttying the floors, while everyone else watched whatever was playing on the Screen. How could you let a grand old lady trip, or allow for her underwear to show?

"George!" a voice ripped through the rooms, as he was stretching to spackle a corner of the dining room ceiling that was nearly beyond his reach. "George?" It was his sister Eleonore, who – he was sure – was on one of the sofas in the library, with another of their sisters, Heather, close by. George put his putty knife in the bin, wiped his hands, and looked down. The worst thing to do was to make a sudden move. He had made that mistake before and plummeted, knocking the wind out of himself. "Easy does it," he said out loud, knowing that no one would hear him, and started down the ladder.

He knew what they wanted. Smiling, he made his way through the Yellow Room, turned left, then right, and continued on through the small foyer that led to the kitchen. He flipped the light switch next to the kitchen door frame, more out of habit than real need. It was not close to being dark out yet. He hadn't even turned on the light in the dining room.

The curtain was swaying, and a pigeon was perched on the sill. The purplish, greyish, greenish markings on its neck mesmerized him. Who knew that pigeons could be beautiful?

They were hungry, and probably thirsty, he knew. And dinner was still hours away. But he had put aside some snacks – leftovers, really, from last night's delivery. He knew his siblings, his parents, and their rhythms.

He never served everything that arrived at 7 p.m. in those anonymous grey boxes that had an address and numbers stamped on them: 311 Prospect Street, 7, 8, 2025 (2), 2045 (3), 2050 (2), 2055 (1). He would carefully store at least half of the meals in the old refrigerator (that he had discovered still worked) in the pantry: sides with sides, on the upper left-hand side of the fridge; entrees with entrees, on the bottom shelf; desserts on the middle shelf. He stored the drinks in the official refrigerator, the one in the kitchen. The dry foods he kept in the cupboards.

It had taken him some time to understand how to store the meals. The delivery people demanded that you return all of the tins that they had brought the day before. In the early days of the new normal, he had tried to keep a couple of them: they were exactly the right size for mixing spackle and putty. But when the delivery people had looked inside the grey box that he had handed them in the enclosed porch at the house's front entrance, the box with the big bold letters STORE TINS AND FOLDED BOXES FOR COLLECTION HERE stamped on it, they saw that there were only 22 tins. "Where are the remaining two?" they had asked through the microphones embedded in their hazmat suits. And with a smile – that he knew no one could see through his mask – George had said, "I must have left them in the kitchen. Why don't I grab the boxes that you have and get the tins back to you tomorrow with today's batch?"

"We will wait," the hazmats had replied, "Just close the door behind you when you go back in." And that, George had understood, was an ultimatum: missing tins, no food. He complied. It made no sense to take a stand.

It took some thinking – and rummaging through the old kitchen cabinets and attic – but he had found a way. He didn't want his family eating all of the food: the entire portions allotted for their breakfasts, lunches, and dinners. It was too much food, too much bad food. – Were they trying to gorge them all? – And he found a way to fix the "bad" part too, some, at least. Pots and pans, salt and black pepper did wonders for broccoli and tofu. The worst of it he just flushed down the toilet.

Searching through the "sides" that he stored in the Tupperware containers with yellow tops – old relics from the days when plastic was still being made and used – George found some broccoli that had been delivered the night before. He pulled out a pot, poured them in, added salt, and went to the "cooking" section of the kitchen.

There was no gas in the stove, of course, and no one had electric cooktops (they taxed the electric grid, or so the new normal had it). But he had discovered that if you re-pipe the water from the radiators you could generate decent heat. All you had to do was add a loop from the feed to the radiator, that is if your grandfather too had loved fixing things and had never thrown out a useful cylinder, coil, plumbing tape, or tool.

He placed four plates on one tray, and three on another as he let the "stove" heat the broccoli. He added glasses, forks, knives, and napkins. He was calculating that Helena and Brad were also with Eleonore. They hardly much moved anymore. Sam, he knew, was with his parents in the Green Room. His mother would never let her first-born – her 'Sammie' – out of her sight for long. They too would be hungry, and thirsty.

He pulled two bottles of water out of the kitchen fridge: one for each tray. He had to move quickly. It was still cold out, and the "stove" was working well. With practiced motions, George turned, grabbed some bread from the old red and white checkered box in the cabinet, and laid a slice on each plate. He turned, headed towards the open window, reached for a towel hanging on the wall next to the radiator, took out the tongs, and clutched the pot with the broccoli. It was hot. Circling back, he went to the trays and laid broccoli stalks on each slice of bread. He poured a bit of "sauce" on each portion, put the empty pot in the sink, filled it with water, took the mask that he had hung on a nail by the sink, and wondered where he should bring the first tray.

It was his constant quandary. Seeing his sisters and brothers sprawled on the couches, watching the images flicker on the Screen was torture. How could Brad, who had thrown the meanest fastball when they were kids on the baseball team, who used once to grip seams all day to strengthen his fingers, have become so soft? And Helena with clean hands? Where were her sculptures?

And Heather's jokes? Her daring to say what no one else dared to think? Her lightning flash jabs were as dried out as Helena's clay. He hadn't heard a laugh in months and months.

But seeing his parents and Sam was almost worse. Their dull looks at the Green Room Screen made him ask himself if his memories of his father playing the piano or hitting a baseball, and of his mother canning tomatoes or sewing a dress, were just dreams. Had there ever been a time when there was music in the air, the smell of fresh food, and light streaming through the open windows? Was the tire swing on the old oak tree really still there? And the cherry trees? The swing set? The gravel, the linden trees, the grill, the roasting pit, the bread oven, the fields and fields of vines?

As he took off his sweater and put on his mask, he decided that he would face his parents first. There was nothing worse than the "Why are you wearing a mask, George? We're not infected, you know!" ritual.

2

George made his way through the rooms with the smaller tray, shivering a bit. The open windows made the big rooms cold. How much smoke would there be this time? he wondered. The smoke. That's what really scared him: the steady stream coming out of the Green Room. It slithered while it was near the floor, and untangled in whisps and tendrils as it rose up towards the ceiling. It almost looked hungry, like it wanted him too.

He could already hear the voices coming out of the screen:

"It was a .33, shot at close range, and the shooter was left-handed," a male voice sentenced. "There is residue on the neck. See?"

"It was clearly a racially motivated crime," a female voice chimed in. "The victim has to have belonged to some racial minority."

"Clearly," the male voice assented. "We should study our charts when we get back to the station."

"Did you get the new ones?"

George nearly tripped as he made his way past the dusty sofas in the hall. It was a big chip in the floor, and he had almost wedged his left foot in it. "Idiot," he told himself. "Pay attention."

"George, is that you?" he heard his mother call out over the screen voices.

"Yes," he said with a smile, firmly believing that they could feel the smile through his voice. "I'm on my way with a surprise for you and Dad. Figured you would be peckish around this time."

There was no response. Only the drone of the screen.

"The victim cannot have been White Caucasian," the female voice solemnly intoned.

"Of course not," the male voice gravely assented.

"There is surely some explanation for this mystery."

The voices were properly weighty. George knew that there would be no sound of another real human voice until his mother noticed the mask.

He walked quietly down the hall and turned right. There they were: his mother, with her Sammie's head on her lap; Sam with a beard, looking like he had spent decades in a drunken stupor; his father, with his grey pants unzipped, his shoes unlaced, and feet resting on the coffee table. "Dad?" George asked, as he walked in, "Dad? Can you move your feet? I've brought you something to nibble on."

"George!" his father said, getting up and reaching for the zipper on his pants, "let me help you with that." George's heart skipped, as it always did when his father actually sounded like his father. There was hope, he thought.

As his father reached out for the tray, his mother exclaimed, "Is that a mask you're wearing, George? Why are you wearing a mask? We're not *infected*, you know!" And the glimmer of movement in his father just died. He slumped back on the sofa like a mechanical toy whose battery had fallen out.

"You know me, Mom," George said with a chipper voice as he laid the tray on the coffee table, "I'm always mixing paints and things. Can't be too careful with chemicals and powders. Am doing the dining room ceiling. Have the ladders out, and pails. You should come and see."

"That's a good boy," his mother purred, as she stroked her Sammie's head "but you've got to rest sometime. Why don't you eat with us? What have you brought?"

"Broccoli," George said, "on bread."

George removed the plates, glasses, and napkins from the tray, and carefully laid formal settings for them. There had to be at least some order in the chaos. "Sam?" he asked as he placed the last napkin to the right of the last knife, "Broccoli?"

"Just give it to me," his mother said. "I'll feed him."

There were faces flickering on the screen: a man and a woman sitting in an indoor café having a conversation. Smoke was streaming out of their mouths.

"I can't do it with you," the woman said, "what you want just can't be done. Think of the poor people if you don't give the Dragon what it wants."

"But, Laura," the man responded putting his hands on hers, "it's my child too. I'll take care of you, both of you. The Dragon can be fed by others."

"You just don't know what you're saying, Mark," the woman sighed looking deeply into his eyes with tears in her own. "How can you? You're just a male, and an egoist. It's all black and white to you. My woman, my child, my life, my pursuit of happiness. Can't you see that we have to think of the common good? To put our own needs beneath the common good? Do you want my mother to be infected, to die, because you refuse to give up your child? Do you want the Dragon to break the windows and doors that protect us when we're at home? Can't you see? Can't you just try to be less male?"

The smoke was getting thicker, as it always did when the images on the Screen spoke of the sacrifice. If the word "infection" increased the dose of smoke, it was at its zenith with the words "male," "body," "dragon," "child," "sacrifice." With them it poured and poured through the screen.

George made for the window wondering how the plot had quickly twisted from a murder scene to the discussion of the sacrifice. The movies, if you could call them that, made less and less sense, unless the point was to push the sacrifice. Someone's death, therefore the sacrifice. Violence, therefore the sacrifice. The new normal's fight on systemic racism, therefore the sacrifice. Gun-shot residue, therefore the sacrifice. A man and a woman at a table together, therefore the sacrifice. Without thinking,

George pulled back the curtain and opened the window and shutters.

"What are you doing?!" His mother shrieked. "Are you trying to kill us all? There's a Dragon out there! It's poisonous!"

George just stood there feeling the light and clean air flowing into the room.

"George!" his mother screamed. "George! The Dragon! The infection! Why should we die?"

"Close that now, George!" his father barked. "You heard your mother."

"But Dad," George pleaded, "I'm just doing what you used to do when we were kids. Don't you remember what you used to say back then, when it was you who opened the windows? 'Change the air in here, kids! Cold air bucks up the immune system.' You're a doctor, Dad. You know about the benefits of light and fresh air. You haven't opened the windows in months. It's dark in here and the air is stale."

A gust of wind blew in as George spoke. He saw the curtains billow and Sam stir. A few more hours, George thought, just a few more hours.

"George!" It was his father again. "You heard your mother! Close that window now."

George just stood there.

"I mean it!" his father said. A hint of his father's old strength was in that voice.

George closed the shutters and window. He pulled the curtain shut. The last time he had tried to get rid of the smoke, they had ripped off his mask. He could still hear his mother screaming, "The mask, the mask! Get his mask!" He remembered what it was like to try to hold his breath that time, even if he knew that they couldn't. It had taken him days to clear his mind.

And to think that Sam had shown signs of life.

He picked up the tray and headed towards the kitchen wondering how he could get fresh air and light into their room without them noticing. A hole in the windows? A pipe? The hall was dark, but he knew the way, where the carpets had curled up, and the sofas loomed. There was a small beam of light seeping through a crack in the large shutter doors. The smoke withered in that beam, its hungry whisps fading.

3.

George put the tray on the kitchen table and picked up the second one. *Move*, he told himself, *just move*. Don't get trapped in your head, in the *what-ifs*, in the *hows*, in the memories, in the unanswerable whys. Just *move*, and keep on *moving*.

He knew he wouldn't recognize himself if he didn't move. When he stopped, his mind would invariably mull over painful memories (or present absurdities), and he would find himself trapped in some "in-head conversation" in which he would finally "tell" those who had wronged him, who had done (or were doing) plainly irrational things, just how stupid or wrong they really were. He would feel the adrenalin course through his veins and his jaw clench when he had those "conversations." And the rage, the seething rage, that pervaded him would make his soul sink deeper and deeper inside of himself. It was like tumbling through a dark rabbit hole, and reality would become harder and harder to recognize: less and less attractive.

"Move," he said out loud, "just move." "A better mask, you need a better mask. Not a fabric one that loops around the ears. You need a mask that they can't rip, or rip off. A gas mask, a full face mask." He forced himself mentally to review the supplies his grandfather had left behind in his workshop. Was there anything there that he could put together to make a gas mask? One of those old-fashioned ones with the see-through plastic eye coverings and huge filters? Did Grandpa have a scuba set?

Making his way through the dining room, and past the piano in the hall, he heard more voices from the Screen. It was the library Screen.

"The Dragon accepted the sacrifice today," a female voice oozed, "and has given one hundred vials of anti-toxin to protect against the infection. One hundred happy people left their homes today to receive it. Our cameras were on location to record the moment. This is Shaneera Smith with Ms. Murphy, at the Otis Center in Victoriaville. Ms. Murphy, how do you feel now that you have received the anti-toxin?"

The library was dark. He could just make out shapes on the couches beyond the arch. "Eleonore," George called. "Eleonore?"

"George?" He heard a voice coming from the floor. "Heather's not moving." George rushed to put the tray on a desk and turn on the lights. Heather was lying face up on the carpet behind the couch. Her eyes were gaping at the ceiling. A whisper of breath dribbled from of her mouth, stirring the smoke that was always thickest when it slithered on the floor.

George headed for the window. It was the smoke, he thought, and the darkness. There were four of them: all closed and shuttered. He would pick up Heather off the floor after he opened them all.

He removed the iron bar from the first shutter, pushed and the wood creaked.

"What are you doing George?" Brad moaned. "Dragon."

George paid no attention to his brother. He pushed again against the shutters with both hands this time, and a third time. They finally gave way and separated. A mass of ice and dirt – guano – fell on the sill and into his hair. He wiped his face and rushed past the arch towards the second window. Light and air were coming in. The smoke, he saw, was red.

"George," Eleonore whispered as he hurried past her, "she's blue."

He lifted the iron bar, put it on the radiator, and pushed, planting his legs, and arching his back. It too was stuck. How many months had it been since they had been opened? There was a flutter of wings. Did the pigeons have a nest on the sill?

"What are you doing George?" It was Brad again.

"Shut up Brad," George snapped back. "Look at Heather."

"It's the infection," Helena croaked. "We've all got it."

"Help me get this open!" George called out, "she'll die from the smoke if we don't."

"I can't," Helena whispered, "I can't even feel my hands."

With a final push the shutters opened. A pigeon flew into the room.

"The Dragon!" Eleonore shrieked from the floor.

George ignored her, glanced at Heather, and made for the third window. Her eyes were still fixed on the ceiling. Eleonore was sitting beside her, rocking back and forth, her arms wrapped around her head. Brad was sprawled on the couch, and Helena was staring at her hands.

"The Dragon has come for the sacrifice," Eleonore sobbed. "Heather! The Dragon."

"Dragon? Sacrifice?" George asked as he pulled the iron bar off the third shutter. "What are you talking about, Eleonore?"

With a second window open, the air was beginning more quickly to clear in the library. The light helped: it dried up the whisps. The pigeon settled on a book on the top shelf, just below the inlaid ceiling. It was cooing. He knew his siblings couldn't see it. It was in the shadows.

"My child gladly gave its life." It was Ms. Murphy of Victoriaville on the Screen. *"It was small, so small. I am so grateful the dragon accepted it."*

George didn't turn to look at the Screen. He knew what he would see: smoke pouring out. "Push," he said, "just push. Then there's just one more."

He felt an arm grab his neck. The elbow was near his ear. "No!" a dull voice said behind him. "I'm not going to let the Dragon in."

The arm was weak, flabby. It felt like an old man's. George didn't move. He wasn't in any real danger, or at least not yet. They were all so frail. It was only when there were more than two of them that they could rip off his mask. They would do so only if they were instructed to. They would react, though, if he moved fast.

"I'm not going to sacrifice my son," Brad whispered in his ear. "The Dragon's not going to rip Heather's belly open."

George let the words sink in. He calmly reached for Brad's wrist, slowly peeled his arm from around his neck, and turned around. "What do you mean, Brad?" he asked fixing his eyes on Brad's. "Brad?"

He didn't need to ask a third time. He knew the answer. He saw it. All of those hours sprawled on the couch with images flickering, the smoke, the dark. They had turned into animals.

Brad covered his face with his hands. George continued to stare at his brother, with his slumped shoulders and flaccid arms. Over his brother's shoulder he saw Helena, who was still staring at her hands. Eleonore, who was still sitting on the floor by Heather, stopped rocking and was looking at Brad. Heather was still staring at the ceiling. Her breathing had become deeper. Her skin a touch pinker. The smoke was clearing.

"It wasn't my fault, George," Brad moaned. "It just happened. You know. . ."

That was when George decided. "You're going to have to find a way of dealing with the smoke, Brad," he said, "and the food. I've left you instructions in the kitchen. Grandma's old fridge in the pantry has the leftovers. The 'stove' I made is in the kitchen. Keep the windows open. Wear a mask when you bring the food. It takes days to clear the smoke from your head."

"What are you talking about, George?" Brad asked. "What smoke? What stove?"

"Just do it, Brad, unless you want the 'in home' service of the *new normal*. It only takes one day of not giving them the tins on time. Read the instructions. They're in the kitchen, on the table."

And with that George turned and headed towards the door. He didn't turn off the lights, close the windows, or worry about the tray. They would have to take care of all of that, or not.

"George," he heard Eleonore whine, her arms wrapped around her head, "but the Dragon ... the infection, Heather."

"I wouldn't worry about the Dragon coming in, or the infection," he replied. "They're already here."

4

It was not that he didn't love the house. He knew it. He knew the quirky wiring and inlaid floors, the hidden faucets, where the walls had been sheetrocked, where the old air conditioners had once been. George stopped one last time to breathe in its proportions: the enameled steel doorframes, the open doors, the staircase, the high ceilings. He gazed at the darker rooms opening behind the doors at the other side of the hall, at the outlines of the books in the tall, tall shelves, the shape of the carob wood desk on the left, the long wing of the piano. The old yearning was still there: the certainty that there was something beyond, and that he was making for it.

He went straight to the closet, got his parka, scarf, and hat. He picked up his knapsack and boots. He continued on to the pantry, pulled some dry food out of the cupboard – cereal, crackers, veggie chips – and some cans. He packed them in his knapsack.

He headed for the kitchen, snatched his sweater and pulled it on. He grabbed a chair, reached for his boots, put them on, and tied the laces. Next it was his parka and hat, his gloves and knapsack.

"Move," he said, "just move," and made his way towards the garden door.

5

It was a glorious day. The sun was shining and the sky was that deep blue that it becomes when it is cold. George could feel the air and light on his face and surrounding him. It was like diving in a pool on a hot summer day. His whole body seemed to relax, even the pores on his face.

And the light. Oh, the light. There was no describing it. After months and months of shadows, the dark, and smoke, the light stunned him, transfixed him, filled him with joy. He straightened up, and just let it come to him.

The cherry trees were still there, he saw once he had convinced himself that he was really outside, and the swing set, the wall in the back, the great oaks, the Cedar of Lebanon. How long it had been since he had seen it, that magnificent trunk that stretched high over the oaks, the Giant of his childhood? Standing at the top of the stairs, he realized just how starved he was for reality: for his own eyes to see trees, his own body to feel the sunlight, his own nose to smell the cedar, his own ears to hear. Everything was still, but he was alive, really alive.

The animals, he saw gazing out at the garden, had taken up living there, or at least rabbits, deer, and squirrels had. Their footprints crisscrossed the snow. There were not that many of them. And maybe, he thought, just maybe, that was why the predators had not yet shown up: the wolves and lynxes. Their footprints were not on the snow, at least not that he could see from where he was standing. It was just a matter of time, he thought, if the rabbits got to work and people continued to stay inside.

The thought of the rabbits brought his golden moment to a screeching halt: Brad and Heather. How could they? What were they thinking? He closed his eyes and could still see his sister lying on the floor blankly staring up. He could still feel Brad's flaccid arm around his neck. He held his breath and clenched his jaw. How could Brad? Helena too?

A door slammed behind him and snapped him out of his head. It was the pantry door. Was it just the wind? Had he closed the garden door?

He wasn't afraid of them coming out. They had been so thoroughly poisoned by the smoke that they wouldn't – or couldn't – leave the house. The voices on the Screen had for months hammered that it was poisonous outside, that they all had to shut themselves up indoors, that they could only go out if they had received the anti-toxin, and that that was not even really safe. With all the smoke that they breathed in, they all believed it.

They could call the police, he realized with a start, and be convinced that they were doing the right thing: 'saving' him from the Dragon and the poison it spread throughout the world. *"Indoors is the common good,"* the Screen droned on and on. *"Think about others. Starve the Dragon!"*

Yes, they could call the police. They didn't even have to dial 911. There was a big red button under every screen. It read POLICE.

Without thinking, George ran down the steps, turned left, and rushed for the gate. He couldn't risk it. If the smallest details of the new normal were enforced as strictly as he knew they were, there had to be protocols in place for those who escaped their homes. Judging from his interactions with the hazmats when they brought the food, or just showed up to ask if there had been demises, to inform him how many lights had been turned on during the week, or to inquire about sacrificial heroes – and instruct him to keep a look out for them – there were protocols, and they were detailed, strict, and decisive.

There was nothing he could do about his footprints, he thought as he ran, at least until he got past the oaks. He could hear the snow crunch under his feet, and feel his muscles. It was good to move, to stretch his legs, to feel his heart pick up speed, to hear his breathing become rhythmic.

He was getting close to the linden trees, the bare linden trees, or at least that is what they called them. George realized that he had never checked if they really were linden trees. They had strange blue berries in the summer that everyone told him were poisonous. Somehow, he couldn't imagine Berlin covered with those strange blue berries. Wasn't Berlin the city with the lane of lindens?

He ducked under their low branches and headed for the cherry trees, where he didn't have to duck, and then on for the oaks behind them. Quickly, more quickly than he thought possible, he saw that the snow was becoming thinner. He had cleared the oaks and was approaching the Giant, the evergreen Giant.

He did not slow down to take in the majesty of the tree. All he could think of was the gate, and that it was close. He thanked God that the gate couldn't be seen from the house, and that his Giant had already hidden his footprints.

The gate, of course, was locked. George had expected that. It had been drummed into them when they were children: lock the gate, always lock the gate. But so too had been where the key was: behind the twelfth brick from the bottom on the left. He had to reach down to pull it out. How things had changed, he thought, since his childhood.

The gate swung open easily. George closed it, locked it, and pocketed the key. That was the new normal, he told himself: anathema in the old one. "Other people might need to open the gate," his father had scolded him the last time he had taken the key. No one trusted in the new normal. No one thought of the next person. It was all about the common 'goo,' as he had come privately to call the "common good" that the Screen kept on harping about. What was that 'goo' anyway? That "common good" that they were asking people to put themselves beneath? To sacrifice their children for? What was it but a longer, lonelier life of terror?

He slowed down his pace to a comfortable jog. He knew the way: he had to go around the walls, make a left, go straight alongside the barchessa – as his mother called the wing his grandfather had built to store the tractors, the wagons, the tools – until he reached the great arch that rose perpendicular to it, and then on down the sloping path that led through the vineyards to the winery.

His footprints didn't bother him anymore. These were his haunts. No one outside the family knew them, and no one really cared about them, especially in winter when there were no grapes, and in a world in which no one dared to go outside.

His feet crunching in the snow soothed him as he jogged past the arches of the barchessa. He could make out the tractors and wagons looming behind them. It was all eerily hushed, deserted, other worldly. "Move," he said, as he always did when memories became painful, and questions flooded his mind, "just move."

Before he knew it, he was at the great arch and saw the vineyards stretching before him: the acres and acres that sloped down to the river. The vines were frozen, the wires between them covered with icicles. At any other time, he might have stopped to take it all in. Everything around him was so clean, so clear, so beautiful: the blue sky, the dark, dark grey – almost black – of the vines, and the white of the snow and ice.

He did not let the thought, or urge, form inside himself. "Move," he said, "just move." He needed somewhere

to sleep, someplace covered, someplace with walls, windows, and a door, someplace he could heat. There was
only one place in the estate that would do: the winery by
the river.

6

The first thing he heard as he ran down the path in the center of the vineyards – other than his own breathing and footsteps – was music. It was faint. He was still a long way off. The vineyards stretched before him as far as he could see: rows and rows and rows of vines. He couldn't even spot the tall trees that lined the river. But there it was: a violin piercing that thick silence that surrounded him, the silence that had fallen over the entire world. It was Bach: the Loure, he recognized, from the Third Partita.

George didn't intentionally slow his pace, but after a few minutes he was jogging in rhythm with the music. It would disappear at times, but just when he thought he had only imagined it, it would pick back up. He didn't forget to listen for other sounds: helicopters, SUVs, wild animals? One never knew who could come after him, or what could attack him.

Nothing came. It was just he, the vineyards stretching all around him, his breathing, the pounding of his heart, the crunching of his feet on the snow, and the violin: the grave, pleading Loure.

The sun was beginning to set. It was becoming bigger, coming closer to the earth, its beams reaching out to the vines, that stood in diagonal lines. Only some of them seemed to receive the embrace. Their icicles sparkled in what looked like joy. The vines to his left seemed altogether silent. Did the sunbeams always touch the same vines? George wondered, as he kept up his jog. Was that how it was? Only some were blessed?

Then he noticed that the beams had moved: the vines that had been sparkling a few minutes before had become quiet, and the ones next to them were being awakened by the light. Of course, he thought, the sun – or was it the earth? – was moving. The arc was closing. Everything would be touched.

It was the earth's motion that allowed everything to be touched. Were the earth not to move, he realized, only some of the vines would be illuminated. The others would be eternally left out. And those in the beam would quickly be burnt. Plants can only take so much direct light.

The air had become orangey pink. No, not pink, never pink. Fuchsia? There was something about pink that bothered George. Was it the word, like "cute," something that was just a cheap imitation of what he saw? That ridiculous color that tasted like bad Moscato?

"Move," George told himself, "just move." He knew that his thoughts, if you could call them that, were keeping him from seeing the wonder that surrounded him, from hearing the violin that once again pierced the air.

7

There was a light in the winery. It was dark, or dark enough for the light to be clearly visible from a distance. George did not stop. There would be no point in stopping, or changing directions. He could not return to the house. Who knew what was going on there . . .

"Move," he said, "just move." He didn't want his mind to be clouded by the slightest hint of Brad and Heather. Was there somewhere else he could go? He forced himself to flip through his memories of the estate.

There was no point in scanning his memories. There was nowhere else he could sleep that night. His grandfather would never have allowed another building on his property. George could just imagine him shrug and ask, "Why waste the good land?"

He could not sleep outside. He had brought nothing to deal with the cold.

The violin picked up again. It was the Gavotte. Still the third Partita, George thought. Whoever was playing knew his Bach. It was loud, or at least louder than it had been.

George's pace picked up, without him noticing. It had taken on the rhythm of the dance. When there were only a few hundred yards left, he killed his doubts. Light or no light, he would go into the winery.

8

He was panting when he opened the door. The air inside was warm. The violin player was plainly in the winery. He could hear the music very clearly. It was the second Minuet. George took a moment to look around. There was enough light to see the shapes of the enormous steel vats in the fermenting room to his right. The rest of that wing – that stretched on and on with more and more vats and barrels upon barrels of wine – was dark and quiet.

He saw the outlines of his grandfather's crest hanging on the wall behind the receptionist's desk. That too was still there. He could make out the contours (or the emptiness) of the corridor to the right of it. How could the player only be on the second Minuet? he suddenly asked himself. He had heard the Loure what seemed like hours ago. He was sure that he had been running much longer than it took to play the Third Partita.

George went to the desk, pulled out the chair, unhooked his knapsack, peeled it off his shoulders, put it on the floor, and sat. He still had to take off his parka, hat, and boots, his scarf, his sweater, and God only knew what else. He would soon start sweating. He was getting hot.

There was only one place the violin player could be, he realized: in the offices. And that made sense. There were sofas in the offices, and a large common room with a kitchen. His grandmother had insisted on it, all those years ago. "You can't expect your men to trudge all the way up to the house for lunch," she had said hands on her hips – or so the story went. "They wouldn't even make it half-way up to the house before the lunch hour was over! Serves you right for making the place so big."

The recollection made him wince. His last memories of his grandmother were of her quietly playing the piano. That was after his grandfather had died, and their son, his uncle Paul, taken over the family business. Paul also had a wife, who had her own way of doing things.

Move, he thought, *just move. Sitting here is not going to make it easier.* He untied his boots, pulled his feet out, and unzipped his parka.

"Hungry?" a voice suddenly said in the darkness.

"Hello?" George answered. "What's that? Who's there?" He stood up and walked towards the voice.

"A friend," the voice said.

"Who are you?" George insisted. It was a male voice. He didn't remember ever having heard it.

"Take off your parka and scarf before you sweat to death," the voice responded. "The closet in the corridor is empty, if you want to hang them up. I'll be in the kitchen."

The music picked up again. It was the Preludio of the Third Partita. The violinist is a master, George thought.

His bowing was quick, precise, and chaste: no deliberate pauses, no stretches of the notes, no bad counting. He turned and walked back to the desk, picked up his boots and knapsack, and headed towards the closet. He was starting to sweat.

He went to the bathroom after he had hung up his parka, scarf, and hat. It was right next to the closet. He put his boots on the rack on the left-hand side of the sink. He had left his knapsack in the corridor to pick up on his way to the offices.

9

The light was coming from the kitchen, and with it the unbelievable smell of roast lamb. The kitchen was the central room in that wing of the winery: its heart. It was big, open, and had high beamed ceilings. In the middle was the island where the magic – as his grandmother had once called it – used to be done, and in which it vanished, with its huge stove, oven, sinks, dishwashers, black granite counters, and pan racks hanging from the ceiling. Perpendicular to it, forming an almost perfect T, was the long oak dining table.

The doors of the offices were on all four of the room's off-white walls. They were simple, polished flame mahogany. Between them stood the cabinets with the tablecloths, the placemats, the napkins, the plates, the glasses, the decanters, the platters, the bowls, the cutlery: everything one needed to eat and serve a meal.

It was exactly as it had been when George had last seen it, including the calendar hanging on the wall. The year was different, of course. But it had the same bright picture of the Regaleali vineyards in Sicily and was crowned by the same Tasca lion. It was opened up to March 2020. The violinist, he saw, was in his uncle Peter's office. Its was the only open door.

George dropped his knapsack by the table and went to the cabinet next to his uncle Paul's office. "Just two plates?" he asked.

"Yes," the voice answered.

He grabbed two simple red and white checkered placemats and the everyday white dinner plates, put them facing each other at one end of the oak table, and went for the cutlery and glasses. "Do I need to get some wine?" he asked.

"It's decanting," came the response from Peter's office.

George looked over and saw the decanter on the corner of the counter. It was filled with that ruby red wine that was his grandfather's pride and joy. The empty Old Vine Zinfandel bottle was, he noticed, in the sink. He took the decanter, put it on the table, and headed for the cabinet with the wine glasses. He chose two for red wine: stemless crystal. "We have nothing to prove," his grandmother always said.

As he was making for the cabinet with the cutlery, the violinist came out of the office and went to the oven. He grabbed mitts hanging under the island, pulled out the lamb, and placed it on the stove. Then came potatoes, that filled the room with a burst of rosemary, brussels sprouts, and fresh bread.

George pulled out three trivets, put two of them on the table and one under the decanter, and headed for another cabinet. A thousand questions raced through his mind as his hands did what they had done countless times since his childhood. Who was this man? And what was he doing in his family's winery? Did he just move in? When? He couldn't have just arrived: he knew the kitchen too well. Where did he get the lamb? Was that really fresh bread?

He knew that he could ask none of his questions. He wasn't even sure that he knew how to speak to people anymore: how to have a normal conversation. Where did one start? He reached out and grabbed a bowl, a platter, and a breadbasket. He paid no attention to what he took.

"I see that you haven't turned on the Screen," he finally said as he brought the serving dishes to the counter.

"And deal with the smoke?" the violinist replied as he reached for knives hanging from the rack above his head. "No thank you. There are enough intoxicated people in the world today. I like clean air, and to open the windows as much as I can. It bucks up the immune system, you know."

A wall fell inside George as the words sank in. "You see the smoke too?" he asked, as he laid the platter, bowl, and breadbasket on the counter, "and what it does?"

"It's there to be seen," the violinist calmly said as he laid out knives, a fork, and spoon. "And worse than it has ever been."

"Bucks up the immune system" echoed through George's head, and "deal with the smoke," "intoxicated." He looked over at the violinist, who was focused on carving the lamb. He needed some wine. He needed to sit, to process. It had to wait. They had to wait, the questions.

He grabbed the bread knife, pulled out a cutting board from the cupboard under the island, and reached for the bread.

"It's hot," the violinist said.

George took a mitt hanging from the island, picked up the bread tin and clapped it upside down on the cutting board. He put the tin in the sink, filled it with water, took off the mitt, hung it, and began to cut the bread.

"Move," the violinist said looking up from the lamb at him, "just move, right?" When his eyes met George's he laughed, a joyous laugh that filled the room.

George just let his hands feel the knife and hot bread. He picked up a slice and lifted it up to his nose. "Bread," he said, "real bread."

Embarrassed, he put the bread in the basket and carried it over to the table. It was *real*, he kept on thinking, *real*. He had forgotten what real was. What real is, he corrected himself. He did not know what was worse: forgetting what the real is, or not knowing how to take it in.

He nearly bumped into the violinist when he turned to make his way back for the other food. "Heads up," the violinist said, "and we need another spoon for the potatoes."

10

He was in uncle Paul's office, the main one, with its huge oak desk, closets, bookshelves, hardwood floors, and private bathroom. The sun was streaming through the open window. George got up with a start and shivered in the cold winter air. He went to the window. The view was the one he remembered, with the willows and birches. The great lawn that sloped all the way down to the river was blanketed with snow.

The sun was bouncing off the river that had turned into a moving tapestry of lights twinkling on a greyish-bluish dancing surface streaked with the deep blue swaths of the undercurrents. There were birds flying over the water, little white birds. They joyfully rose and swooped, chasing each other.

George was captivated by the deep blue swaths in the river. The dance of the shimmering lights was engulfing them. Were the undercurrents joining in on their laughter? Would the whole river rejoice?

Coffee, he suddenly thought. Had he made it the night before? He turned, made the bed, folded it into the sofa, put his pillow in the closet, pulled on his jeans and shirt, and made for the door.

The kitchen was empty. There was no sign of the dinner. Uncle Peter's office emanated light. The window must be open in there too, George thought.

He headed towards the refrigerator (refrigerators, really: there were four in the island in the center of the room), his bare feet making the only sound that he could hear. He opened the fridge on the far right. In the front and center of the top shelf he saw his Philadelphia mug, the one they had given him when he went to visit his aunt all those years ago. It was full. So too was the refrigerator. It was stocked with milk, butter, jam, cheese: things he hadn't seen in months.

He took the coffee, and a sip, while the refrigerator door was closing. The same overwhelming rush of flavor and scent that he had felt the night before washed through him. All he could think was real.

He had a memory flash: "This is not a new war," the violinist had said when they were at the table. "It is as old as time. It is the war of what is versus what I want."

He could only recall disconnected feelings, images, sounds from the dinner: the overwhelming feeling of fullness, realness, Grace, the joy of the flavors, discussing the smoke, the hazmats, Brad . . . hearing "Do not fear... just walk, let the path come to you," "Let in the light, accept it," "Rejoice." It had all made sense to him then.

He headed for the table, pulled out a chair, and sat. There was a full breadbasket waiting for him, and a note. A ray of light coming from uncle Peter's office illuminated it. The handwriting was quick, precise, chaste:

Do not chase the dragon, let it come for you. It will come. It wants you. Its desire is for everyone. It does not often show itself. It prefers the dark. It slithers. You cannot defeat it alone.

Do not fear. Do not arm yourself.

Let in the light. Learn to see, to rejoice. The path is there for you to walk. You are not alone.

George stood up and looked around the kitchen for something to do. Prophetic tones bothered him. He had had nothing to do with the Dragon. Why would he chase it? Why should he not arm himself? He had successfully defended himself against the smoke and screens, hadn't he?

The surfaces were pristine, even the pans glistened. The memory of the violinist saying, "Move, just move, right?" and filling the room with a joyous laugh burst into his mind. He turned. He had heard the laugh.

His heart began to pound. He held very still. He was afraid of hearing a response.

When he finally let out his breath, he picked up his mug. He took another sip of coffee, could no longer taste it, put the mug back in the fridge, and, turning his back to his uncle Peter's office, headed for the other wing.

He could make out the sofas in the room behind the receptionist's desk – the hallway, really, that he had crossed the night before, when he had followed the light and the smell of lamb. He almost yearned for the house: getting up in the morning, making his bed, grabbing his coffee, showering, serving breakfast, going to his restoration plan, working on whatever project was next, serving more food, spackling, answering the door, storing the meals, serving more food. There were no questions in the house. He had always noticed the hundreds of little things there that needed fixing, and had always wanted to fix them. He loved the house.

II

It had been a turbulent time when the Dragon came on the scene. It had started with a tidbit: a Dragon had appeared in a far-off land and people were dying. No one, experts sentenced, other than those who lived near its lair, was in danger. It was an odd soundbite, that no one mentioned, not even in passing, until a second mass death site was reported. A flurry of information about the Dragon then began suddenly to dominate all broadcasts, all conversations.

The Dragon was infecting people, the experts pronounced: those who breathed in the Dragon's breath became deathly ill. Images of the dying began to circulate. But *It* could be contained, they said: *Its* lairs circumscribed. A third mass infection site was then reported, and a fourth. "Stay indoors," the experts began to say, "stay safe. *It* can be contained."

News broke that the infected, the "breathers," too could transmit the infection. "Stay indoors," the experts repeated louder. "Stay safe. Watch for symptoms! Distance yourselves!" Then the experts screamed that the "breathers" could be asymptomatic. "You cannot know," they shrieked, "who the 'breathers' are!" Everyone was a threat.

They were showered with orders: the mask order, curfew orders, the orders to close all windows, lockdowns, the order to appoint someone to accept food deliveries, to be ready at any and all times to open the doors to the hazmats. The orders were accompanied by a steady stream of numbers and warnings: the number of people who had died from exposure to Dragon breath, of "breathers," of hospital beds occupied, the warning that hospitals could reach capacity. Whispers of trucks filled with bodies driving to remote places under the cover of night and hasty mass graves began to circulate.

There was hope, they were suddenly informed by breathless politicians in a post replete with emoji rainbows: "the Dragon will negotiate, if everyone complies!!" Hourly updates on the negotiations appeared on all media sites and networks.

"Dragon will supply anti-toxin" a brief post pasted with multicolored praying-hands-emojis announced.

"The Dragon wants children," the next brief post read. "Team has left negotiation site." It only had one emoji: the crying face with a single tear.

Hours passed. "People demand anti-toxin," followed by the red angry-faced emoji was suddenly plastered on all sites, followed by,

"Protesters organizing" and a picture of an angry mob.

"Team seeks volunteers to promote the 'common good,'" then appeared with the haloed-smiley-face emoji.

"GAME-CHANGER: DRAGON WILL ACCEPT THE UNBORN" was the final post. It had a picture of a group of smiling politicians shaking hands.

Networks hailed the winning team and lined up to interview its members. "Managing to convince the Dragon to accept the unborn was a real game changer," a silver-haired man with a toothy smile sentenced. "They're not really human, are they?"

George had taken everything in stride. Having to stay at his parents' after the family reunion – the sudden prohibition to leave whatever house and town one was in came months after news of the Dragon had first appeared – was a relief. It gave him a much-needed break from his City work: a chance to get his bearings.

He had left his phone in his apartment – and given the strict order not to contact him. He always did when he went to the house. He could not interact with his family if he used his "work mind." He could not work if he used his "family mind." Moving meant keeping the worlds distinct: answering Sam's "What do you think of X company?" (that would invariably be accompanied by a torrent of indecipherable claims about X) with a smile and shrug.

As the days stretched into weeks, he had turned to the house. Caring for it had given him a path to walk throughout the chaos and radio silence from his office. It had let him tune out the smoke in the house and destruction outside of it: what it meant, what it portended.

He had tried to get his siblings to join in on the work. "We are all in danger," his mother had moaned. "One of you, at least, should be chosen for the anti-toxin! The names come out every hour on the hour." His siblings had diligently watched for their names and assured their mother that it was she who deserved it.

12

Now here he was out of the house, alone, walking through the silent winery that had refrigerators filled with things he had not seen in months, notes written by violinists, hearing laughter in an empty room, and no plan. How was he to *move*?

George headed for the windows and great rear door that led unto the grand stone terrace with its breathtaking view of the river. He could feel the carpet under his feet. Everything was as it had been when he was last in his grandfather's domain. He opened the window and pushed back the shutter. A burst of light and cold air flooded the room, and with it a voice. "Look, Daddy, look," it called. And then came a male voice – "Now, that's what I call a snowball!" – followed by an exultant squeal.

George hungrily searched over the snow-covered lawn beyond the terrace, almost wishing his grandfather's vision had not been so big. Who were they? Where were they? Was the Violinist there? He rushed to another window and threw open the shutter. Its bang was met with another squeal. "Look, Daddy, look! a man! A man, Daddy, look!"

There! he finally saw them, by the weeping willow on the right. It was Peter, "Junior" as he was known, and a little girl. They were packing snow.

Junior stood up. "George," he called out waving. "George? Is that you?"

"Junior!" George called back. "Wait! Wait there. I'm coming out!"

He closed the windows and rushed to the closet. He threw on his parka, grabbed his gloves, and headed to the bathroom for his boots, trying to zip up his parka as he moved. What was Junior doing here? he asked himself, and what was his daughter's name? His wife's? He pushed open the bathroom door, switched on the light, grabbed his boots, and sat on the toilet to tie their laces, not even noticing that he had no socks.

He ran towards the great rear door, opened it, and pulled back the locking bars on its enormous shutters, grateful that he had put on his gloves. He remembered his skin sticking to the bars all those years ago when he and his grandfather had spent a night in the winery over the Christmas break.

There was another child, he saw, once he made it past the terrace, down the stairs, across the lawn, and over to the willow. Two little ones huddled around Junior.

"Welcome, George!" Junior said with a grin and hug. "Kids," he called out, "come on over. Cousin George is here, the City boy, the big man. Remember? His parents live up at the big house."

George looked at the little ones taking him in with wide eyes under their woolen caps. He heard the footsteps of others bounding over the snow. He recognized the big ones, who were running: Michael and Gabriel (who had to be around 10 and 11?), and Anne was it? and Cecilia, who had to be around 7 and 8?

"Was it you who came in last night, George?" Junior asked, picking up the little girl.

"Yes," George heard himself say. "You were here?"

"With these rascals," Junior said beaming at the little boy to his left.

"Not just us, Daddy," the little girl piped up.

"George," Junior said as he smiled at the little one in his arms, "I don't believe you know Sarah. You remember Gabe and Mike though, don't you? And Anne and Cece?" The big ones had just gotten there.

George nodded, trying to take in the sight.

"This little goat here, on the other hand," he said reaching out to rub the child's head, "is George. We call him 'Little George.' He likes numbers too, and fixing things. He's always asking how Great-Grandfather did this, or Great-Grandfather did that! He has big dreams of conquering the world: of cleaning it up and setting it straight. Remind you of someone?"

13.

It was an immense greenhouse crowned by a glorious glass vault. Broccoli was growing, and brussels sprouts, beans, peas, arugula... Tens of children were playing what looked like tag, between countless vegetable beds studded with neat rows and rows of plants. They had all made their ways to it together, trudging over the snow, Mike and Gabe throwing the occasional snowball, Sarah peeking out at him.

George gawked. The place dwarfed the garden atria in the grand City skyscrapers. Only the covered gardens in Singapore could compete with it.

"It was really Beth," Junior said as they walked through what seemed to be the core of the building: a common room that looked like a broader squattier version of the winery's kitchen. "She was the one who convinced Dad and uncle Paul to build her a separate wing, if you can call a building bigger and taller than the main one – we have a second floor with living quarters, the door's behind that door over there – a wing!"

"That was years ago," Junior continued as he opened another door, "while you were in the City making the big money. Cheese and organic produce were becoming the thing then, remember? And Beth wanted in on them."

George tuned out Junior's excited talking and stared at the new room. It too was huge and crowned with an enormous glass vault, but looked like a meadow dotted with bleating goats and sheep, cows, calves, shrubs, trees, and heaven knew what else. There were people too: adults milking cows, tending shrubs, laughing.

"Cheese and wine, she told the bosses," Junior beamed, "are a natural combination, and greens too... She had shown them plans, the most intricate plans I've ever seen, all the way down to the nuts and bolts. So this operation just sort of fell in place. Before we knew it, we were living here with the kids, literally!"

14

He hadn't realized how hungry he was until they sat down at one of the tables in Beth's common room. They had walked the length of Beth's cellars, past rooms and rooms of cheese and hay, dried fruit, bags and bags of wheat, dehydrators, desiccators, mills, carders, spinners, freezers, and ramps, through the tunnel that connected Beth's wing to the winery, and then past barrels and barrels of wine and brandy, up the staircase into the fermenting room, on to the winery's reception room.

"It's lunch time!" Junior had suddenly said. "Can't be late."

George did not know how many of them there were, where they all came from. He could hear their voices making that wave-sound that fascinated him whenever he paid attention to it. The children struck him, all of those children sitting with their parents at all of those tables: squirming, laughing, reaching for bread. Had he ever seen so many children?

He knew he must look dazed. "You got in last night, I heard," he caught a man next to him – Mark? – suddenly ask. George turned to him. The sound of a fork clinking on a glass saved him from having to answer. Junior stood up. Chairs scraped the floor, parents shushed their children. They all stood, bowed their heads. "Bless us, O Lord," he began. They all added their "Amens."

"One more thing," Junior added, "Welcome George, my cousin. He arrived last night." They all clapped.

The meatloaf was exquisite, and the beans. The trifle otherworldly.

15

There was coffee in the fridge. He had made it himself at Beth's, the night before, to the amazement of those who were cleaning the common room when he had shown up. "Coffee now?" a kind lady in pink, who was polishing the counter, had asked him. "How will you be up in time for the Angelus?"

George hadn't understood the question. "It's for tomorrow morning, Ma'am," he had said. "I drink it cold."

"Bless you!" she had replied with a beaming smile, wiping her hands on her floral apron and stretching out the right one for him to shake. "It's Rebecca. And don't you worry about remembering my name. You were crushed with new faces today. You must be overwhelmed, though I would be surprised if you, with your mind and all, haven't already memorized well-nigh more than half of our names!"

"The coffee's under there," she had then added picking up her rag and getting back to her cleaning, "Ground and unground. The grinder too."

"There?" George had asked.

She had laughed, put down her rag, and walked over to him. "There I go again, expecting people to understand my shorthand," she had said. "Here. Let me show you."

Yes, George thought as he looked out the window on the river quietly flowing, coffee was in the refrigerator. He had seen no sign of smoke, he mulled, no Screen, no mask, felt no fear as he wandered through Beth's wing the previous afternoon. People had nodded at him, presented themselves, asked if he needed anything, and gone about spinning, weaving, making bread, cheese, and whatever else they were doing: focused, busy, smiling. The aromas had been intoxicating.

The winery kitchen had felt empty when he had gotten back in. He had pulled out the leftovers and decanted a bottle of the winery's cabernet, that had not tasted as it ought. He had seen no sign of the Violinist, but had set a place for him. His note was still there on the table, and the breadbasket. He had washed up, looked out the window, made his bed, and slept: deep dreamless sleep.

The sky was grey, when he woke: swollen with moving clouds. The bare trees stood. George took it all in from the window, as he mulled. *Quietly flows the quiet Don* came to mind.

16

Little Sarah had fallen asleep in his arms. She had just shown up that morning in uncle Paul's office as George watched the river and reflected. She had walked up to him and put her hand in his. Then she had taken him to her lambs, her calves, the raspberries, her secret hideouts, her bedroom. "Careful with the stairs, Big George," she had warned as they went to her quarters. "Always hold on to the railing. You don't want to fall!"

When the bell rang, she put her hands together and said, "Big George, stop! Stand still! It's the Angelus!" They'd lunched together and gone for a walk outside. She'd scolded him when the bell again had rung. They had been back inside, in the meadow. "Put me down, Big George!" she had said. "It's the Angelus. We belong to God!" Once she was on her feet, she crossed herself. He joined her prayers. She had sat next to him at dinner.

They were having a quiet brandy in Beth's living room. "So how are things out there really?" Junior asked.

George let his mind wander back to the Screens, the hazmats, the smoke, the darkness. He looked down at sleeping Sarah. Did Junior know that people were holed up, intoxicated, gorged with insipid food, and were sacrificing their children?

"There was a violinist here the night I came," he finally said after taking a sip of brandy, minding not to wake Sarah. "I didn't see him today, or yesterday. Did he just leave?"

"Violinist?" Junior asked shaking his head. "People come through the front door of the winery all the time. We hear the bell chime in the wing. We leave them alone for a while. Don't know of a violinist. Can ask, though. You came on Sunday, right? That's when we put the kids to bed early and stay in our quarters. Your violinist could have come and gone without anyone noticing. It's for people like him that we don't lock the front door."

George remembered the unlocked door. Junior was living by the old rules, he realized, the rules that forbade putting the gate key in your pocket, and locking the winery, in case Grandma wanted to drive down to pick up Grampa who was overworking. He could not tell a person, who lived according to traditions established by people long dead, about the Screens, smoke, hazmats, about his father with unzipped pants flopping on the couch, about Brad and Heather.

He took another sip of brandy.

Beth came in with a smile and kiss for Junior. She was carrying folded clothes. Shoes dangled from her hands. She let the shoes fall to the floor, put the clothes on the coffee table, and neatly straightened the shoes. "Finally!" she said, as she sat, kicked off her own shoes, and curled up her legs on the couch. "Junior, give me a sip of that?"

There was something solid about Beth, George thought, something real. Her socks, sweater, and jeans were somehow simply elegant. Her eyes sparkled. She could see the world around her, George knew, and pick up on what was missing. He just watched her, absorbed her presence.

"So little Sarah has taken you under her wing," she laughed, meeting his glance. "She's quite something: just finds a way of soothing things. The animals love her. She always shows up when they're giving birth."

George looked down at the little girl in his arms: her total abandon, her trust, her peace. There wasn't a single tense muscle in her. She emanated acceptance and hope. He smiled. He couldn't help himself.

"I don't think you would recognize life out there, Junior," he said quietly, not taking his eyes off little Sarah, "I doubt that anyone can. It is the farthest thing from this."

"You're going to need a change of clothes, George," Beth said pointing at what she had brought, "and shoes. I think you're about Junior's size, right? They're for you."

He couldn't help thinking of Sarah and her warning about the railing as he made his way down the stairs, clothes in arm. He couldn't help smiling. He nodded at a couple on its way up. "Good night," they said, "God bless." "Good night," he said, and continued so to greet people all the way through the tunnel.

17

The snow on the driveway was pristine. There were two driveways, really: the old one for the shipment of wine and delivery of bottles, corks, boxes, and whatever else was needed to package wine, and the new one for Beth's wing. They were both wide, long, windy. George didn't know if they connected, or where, he suspected was more likely the case. He knew that they both eventually led to the highway. He was on the winery's. He watched the sunrise and could not see it. The nightmare was still hovering in his mind.

He had been at the large window behind the desk in his office, alone, overlooking the City. There was no one on the streets: only flocks and flocks of birds. Suddenly the Dragon appeared and landed on the skyscraper across from him. He watched the building crumble under the Dragon's weight: implode in a cloud of dust that extruded people and debris. With a beat of its wings, the Dragon then rose and landed on the sky-scraper next to it. It too imploded, and with that same cloud of dust, people, and debris. And the Dragon rose again, and landed on another skyscraper, that turned into a cloud of dust, and then on another, and another, and another, until the only thing George could see was rubble, rubble and the Atlantic. There were people trapped under that rubble.

He had awakened in a pool of sweat, jumped out of bed, quickly showered, dressed, and rushed out of the winery. The front door was still unlocked. "Move," he had said out loud, "just move."

He had taken a run to the river, trying to drive the images out of his head. He had tried to force himself to remember the date of the last time he had gone fishing with his grandfather, the kind of fishing rod he had used, the kind of bait.

The "moving" hadn't helped. The Dragon and the rubble had "moved" with him: the images in the dream playing and playing in his mind. He had stopped running when he had heard the river. "Calm down before you kill yourself," he had ordered. "Think! Wake up!" He had stared into the darkness, felt it, and slowly made his way back to the driveway, where he watched the sunrise that he could not see.

He could feel the rage growing inside him. He wanted to howl, scream, break something. The words *urbs aeterna* flitted through his mind, the eternal city: Rome. He snorted. Rome was no more eternal than the Great Wall of China impregnable. He had seen Roman ruins all over the Mediterranean. Civilizations end, and that, he told himself as he began to walk, was just a fact. They collapsed, like the skyscrapers. So what? "What difference does it make if it's the City's turn?" he asked, out loud. "Why do you care?"

A bird squawked in the distance. George stopped. "Damned birds," he said. The stillness mimicked the eerie emptiness of the City in his dream. A memory flashed through his mind as he scanned the silent, frozen world: the Violinist saying, "This is not a new war. It is as old as time. It is the war of what is versus what I want."

"I want," echoed in his head, "*what is* versus what *I want*." George sucked in his breath, glanced at his grandfather's winery, and began again slowly to walk. His mind went back to Rome, and the last time he had been in the Colosseum: the disgust he had felt then feeding his rage. What civilization can survive on bread and circuses, he barked inwardly, on calling for more and more foreign mercenaries to do the fighting, and on leaving the working to the provinces, so that those addicted to the gore of the gladiator fights that the Caesars paid for could sit and rot?

It was the *I want* that had mattered to them, all of them, he suddenly saw. The Caesars weren't interested in the facts, the well-being of the people, culture, civilization. They had ignored them. They had enslaved the people by gorging them, just so that they could focus on their own *I want*. And the people had let themselves be enslaved: stuffed as they were with what to each was *I want*. Facts, civilization, their own real well-being had meant no more to them than they had to the Caesars. It was their next high that counted.

Latin verses began to fill his mind: "*Persicos odi, puer, adparatus*" – I hate Persian trappings, boy; "*Nunc in quadriviis et angiportis. . .*" – now in the intersections and the dark alleys. . . Rome, the Romans had been so intoxicated by what I want that they hadn't even realized they were getting fat.

"No!" he said stopping again. "*Qualis artifex pereo!*" had popped into his mind, Nero's last words: "What artist dies in me!" Nero, the lyre player, who had burnt down Rome in order to build his Rome. The Caesars hadn't ignored the facts, the people, civilization – what is – he saw. They didn't *want them*. They wanted to replace *what is* with their what *I want*. Nero had used the fire ruthlessly: to rebuild, to persecute.

They were in danger, he understood in a flash: the crumbling City marked the beginning of something far, far worse. Its desire is for everyone. . . It was on the table, in the kitchen: in the note. He had to do something: he couldn't just sit and watch. George began again to walk, his mind reeling.

"And what of your *I want*?" a voice inside him suddenly asked.

He froze. My *I want*? he asked. To succeed, he automatically answered. The lyrics of the old song flooded his mind – "I want to be a part of it . . . the city that never sleeps" – and with it the skyline at night, Avery Fisher Hall, the little pizza place on John Street, Beekman, the

Apthorp, landing at LaGuardia at night when it felt like the airplane would land in the water: the energy, the feeling of accomplishment. His heart swelled. "Yes," he said, "I want to be a part of it," of the City that never sleeps.

A powerful wave of nostalgia washed through him, for the illuminated buildings reaching up to the night sky, for the snaking lights on the streets below them, for the dinners at Le Bernardin's, at Keens, breakfast at Balthazar's. What was his I want? To be a part of it again.

The horror of his nightmare burned in him anew: watching the Dragon tear it all down. He wanted to run. He knew that it was useless. It was gone, all gone. He howled.

The sun was rising higher. Had he lifted his eyes he would have seen that the winery his grandfather had built was aglow. He could not. All he could see was the destruction. He began again to walk.

"What is the *it*?" the voice inside him asked. "What is the *it* that you want to be a part of?"

The it? George asked, puzzled. "It" was the City, of course, the concerts, restaurants, drinks: his home.

"What is the *it*?" the voice inside him insisted. "*What is* the *it* that you want to be a part of?"

The question irritated him. Did he have to spell out the obvious? The "it" was exactly what he wanted to feel again: engrossed, challenged, accomplished. The "it" was being in the office, poring over graphs, reports, projected budgets, making forecasts of companies' growth and profitability:

of their earning power. The "it" was meeting with people, deciding what company would be financed, ensuring that the funds were released. The "it" was entertaining new proposals, ordering that data be gathered, poring over them, making forecasts. The "it" was celebrating at gala openings, in exotic places, or on helicopters flying to yachts sailing in the Mediterranean. The "it" was living in his world, with its rituals and rhythms, knowing that he was in control. The "it" was moving. The "it" was normalcy.

"*What is* the *it*?" the voice inside him demanded. "What is the **it** that you want to be a part of?"

George stopped. "It?" he asked, as in "existing thing?" What "existing thing" did he want to be "a part of?"

His City life flashed before his eyes. None of it, not the data nor the forecasts, not the meetings nor the celebrations had had anything to do with "existing things," with the reality of the companies whose future he had helped forge (or break): their products, the people who made them, the places where they were made, the people who bought them, their authentic needs.

The *real* had been the forecasts that he, they, had made for companies (and banks) and their realization: the volume of exchange and profit. The *real* had been the faces, those same old faces that he saw in D.C., the Forbidden City, at Victoria & Albert's or wherever else he and they (and they with whom he had made and imposed forecasts) had met.

There were no "its" in what he wanted. No existing things.

"It" was a virtual world that fed itself. They had made the revenue projections; they had decided how much profit was enough (and it was never enough); they had gathered the data – the actual volume of exchange, margins of profit; they again projected; they had gathered the data; they had again projected . . .

"It" was *I want*: his *I want*, their *I want*.

"It" was a ravenous *want*.

For their virtual world to be, they had to convince people that they – the "magic they" who worked in the high-sounding offices of global finance – were talking about the real world. Investors believed them. They bought and sold that stock that their reports said to buy and sell. Politicians, schools, private citizens believed them. They staked their futures on their reports.

They, the "magic they" had seduced them: teased out each individual *I want* and tethered it to their giant *I want*. You can be a part of it, they had whispered: *progress*. They hadn't only coaxed them into investing in the companies that they had chosen. They had seduced them into buying more and more of their companies' products, products that broke ever more swiftly. Maximizing profits required making money circulate.

"They" did end up talking about "existing things," in a sense, he saw with horror. They convinced big players to relocate industries to foreign countries. They tethered the common man – who had fewer and fewer children (they were 'too expensive') – to pay fortunes to send them to college so that they might have a spot in their world.

They, the "magic they," had turned *what is* into their giant *I want*.

He couldn't breathe. It had all become dark. He saw the tendrils that he had woven throughout the years, luring people into the giant *I want*. Was that why he had taken to prodding himself to *move, just move*? Did he know that if he stopped moving, he would see the giant *I want* in which he lived twisting *what is*: that they were remaking reality? So he would not notice that he was changing stone into bread?

Did he think he was some kind of saint for feeding his family, restoring the house? What a joke! He was worse than all of them. His world's giant *I want* had become the world's *what is*.

He felt a hand reach for his. George looked down. It was Sarah in her nightgown. Her feet were bare. Her lips were blue.

"George," she said, "cold."

George reached down and picked her up. "Sarah!" he cried out. "Sarah what are you doing here?"

She put her head on his shoulder. "Cold, George," she whispered.

He turned and ran back to the winery holding her as tightly as he could. He could feel her bouncing in his arms. She was shivering. Her teeth were chattering. Water, hot water, was all he could think. Rub her feet. Cover her with blankets. Please no, he pleaded, no.

He rushed through the front door, kicked it closed, and on to his uncle Paul's office, grabbed some blankets in the closet, and wrapped her in them. She was shivering. He took her in his arms and sat on the sofa swiftly running his palm up and down the blankets to generate heat, reaching for her feet, rubbing them, blowing on them. Body warmth, he remembered. He quickly put Sarah down, unzipped his parka, unwrapped the blankets, and picked her up again, holding her close.

The shivering stopped. Her lips were becoming red. "Sarah," he finally asked in a whisper, "Sarah, what were you doing outside?"

She had fallen asleep. The same look of total abandon, peace, and trust were on her face. The same acceptance, the same hope emanated from her.

"George?" a voice broke into his sleep. "George?" He was sitting on the couch with Sarah in his arms. He looked up. It was Junior standing in the door of Paul's office. "Thank God! Beth was right. Sarah's with you," he said. "We need your help."

18

"*Fiat mihi secundum verbum tuum*" – let it be done to me according to thy word – George said with the whole community. It was the noon Angelus, and Junior was leading the prayer. George looked around at the children and their parents. They were in the greenhouse. They had all been picking beans – the help that Junior needed was with harvesting a bumper crop – when the bell rang. Everyone had stopped what he was doing, bowed his head, and made the sign of the Cross.

Little George, at his side, was fidgeting. He didn't know what to do with the beans in his hands. George reached out with his left hand palm up for them. Little George dropped them in it with a serious face, quickly crossed himself, and carefully joined his flat hands together with his fingers pointing up.

"*Fiat mihi secundum verbum tuum*" – let it be done to me according to thy word. The words exploded in his head as he intoned "*Sancta Maria, Mater Dei ora pro nobis. . .*" – Holy Mary, Mother of God, pray for us... What did they mean? "Let it be done to me." It was important. Everything revolved around that "*Fiat mihi*," somehow.

He knelt with them – noticing that Little George had carefully placed his left hand on his left thigh, mirroring his own movement – for *"Et Verbum caro factum est"* – and the Word became flesh.

Beth hadn't let it be done to her when she had willed the wing into existence, George's mind protested as he once again recited, *"Sancta Maria, Mater Dei..."* – Holy Mary, Mother of God. She had "wanted in" on the "organic" thing. She had planned the place "down to the nuts and bolts," as Junior had said, bursting with pride that first day. And George could well imagine just how much she had had to push to get the place built: to make budget projections, counter objections. From what he had seen of Beth, George suspected that she had supervised every detail of its construction, from the sketching of the first drafts, to the giving of the last coat of paint. He could just see her with a hardhat on her head – a yellow one, he imagined, for some crazy reason – driving an excavator herself. Yet here they were praying, let it be done to me.

"So that's the famous Big George thinking face!" he heard Beth say with a laugh at his side as he made his way to lunch.

George turned to look at his *cousin-in-law?*

"The Big George thinking face," Beth said again, her eyes sparkling. "Junior has been saying it for years: 'Little George has the Big George thinking face.' He's right!'" Then, stretching out a hand that was full of beans, she added, "A bean for your thoughts."

George stared at Beth. "I make a face when I think?" he asked.

"And you can't hear either," she grinned. "Just like you, Little George!" she added, caressing her son's face. "Sneaking up on you two was child's play. What has you so engrossed?"

He wasn't used to direct questions about himself or his thoughts. Direct questions about work were simple. Their parameters (and consequently responses) were clear. Direct questions about himself confounded him. How was he supposed to respond to "How are you?" He didn't have an internal MRI, and certainly couldn't tell if he was sane or insane. He couldn't see himself to analyze himself while he looked at himself. All he could see when he tried was himself looking at himself, trying to see himself. In college he had learned to deflect "How are you?" He would laugh and say, "I was asking myself the same question. How about you?" That seemed to do the trick.

Here, then, was Beth asking him what "had him so engrossed." He didn't want to deflect. He also couldn't help wondering if he was making the face again, and how she could have the patience to wait for him to come to grips with a question to which most people could immediately respond.

"It was the Angelus," he finally said. "I was thinking about the Angelus."

"And what did the genius not understand?" Beth immediately asked, nudging him with her shoulder.

"*Fiat mihi*" – "Let it be done to me" – George responded without thinking about the question, or paying attention to the storm in his mind.

Beth smiled, that radiant smile that filled him with joy. "I can see why that would bother you," she laughed. "How could *the* man of action not be bothered by *Fiat mihi*?"

George was bewildered.

"Come on, George," she coaxed, tilting her head, "we all read for years about you playing the big game, hobnobbing with the greats. Junior, Pete, and Uncle Paul were so proud! They would show me pictures of you looking like a million dollars at the Met Opening Gala, at the big meet in the Forbidden City, in Dubai, and God only knows where else you went."

He couldn't respond.

She leaned in and, standing on tiptoes, whispered, "George, you were a player, one of the ones who called the shots, who determined the fates of economies and people, until this whole Dragon thing, at least. How could a player not be flummoxed by *Fiat mihi*?"

George felt himself blush and cringe at the same time. Images of the galas, meetings, his dream, crumbling skyscrapers, rubble flooded his mind. He lowered his gaze. Proud of him? Did she understand what she was saying about him? Did she know what "they" had done? What "they" were still doing? What he would be doing, had he not gone to that family reunion those many, many, many months ago. He would not have been stuck indoors avoiding the smoke – or in a magic world he hadn't even known existed – had he not gone to his father's birthday party. How could she be smiling at him?

He felt a hand softly reach for his arm. "I've touched a nerve," Beth said. "Sorry."

19

He was on Little George's tour of Beth's wing. They had gone to the chapel, the classroom. "This is my favorite part, Big George," Little George said as he led him to the math section in the library.

George looked on in wonder, and not just because a 5-year-old had a favorite part of a library, or that it was the math section. The collection was extraordinary. There were Euclid's *Elements*, of course, but also Riemann's *On the Hypotheses Which Lie at the Bases of Geometry*, Gödel's *On Formally Undecidable Propositions of Principia Mathematica and Related Systems*, Frege, Nöther, Dedekind, Russell, Cantor.

"Can you read this with me?" Little George asked. It was a book George had never seen: *Emmy Noether: The Most Important Mathematician You've Never Heard Of*. Without waiting for him to answer, Little George took the book, signed the sheet at the end of the shelf, took George's hand, and led him past tables where people were silently reading, to a corner by the window. "We can read here," he said. "This is the talking corner." He pulled out a chair at a little table, turned on the light – though the sun was streaming through the windows – and sat. George sat on the floor.

Little George opened the book and began to read from the inside jacket cover. "How do you say this word?" he asked after he had read "brilliant mathematician who made re..." and looked up at George.

"Revolutionary," George replied.

"No, Big George," Little George protested.

"Help me read it. 'Re' and then?"

"Vo," George said, and Little George repeated it.

"Lu"...

"And what does 're-vo-lu-tio-nary' mean?" Little George asked.

George hadn't realized that reading with Little George really meant listening to him read and helping him sound out (and understand) words that he wasn't able to read. He caught on quickly.

They had sounded their ways through "my-ste-ry," "ac-cept-a-ble," "oc-cu-pa-tion," "u-ni-ver-si-ty," and tens and tens of other words, defining them, discussing them, when George heard other voices in the library.

"George, you here?" It was a child. "George?"

Little feet scampered.

"I'm here with Big George," Little George answered.

Four faces popped out from behind the bookcases and quickly at the table.

"Big George," Little George solemnly said, "this is Adam," pointing to a red headed boy on the right "and this is Tommy," pointing to a little dark-haired boy. "This is Theresa," and pointed to a little girl who was eating an apple, and "This is Daniel."

The children all held out their hands. George stood and shook them one by one, including Theresa's sticky one.

"What are you doing?" Theresa asked.

"Math," Little George responded, showing them all the book.

"Can we do math too?" she asked.

"Yeah!" Tommy said, "Math!"

George cringed, wondering how he could help four children learn to read at the same time. "What do you usually do together?" he asked, looking for an escape.

"Play," Adam, who looked like he wanted no part of books or math, responded.

"Then why don't you all go and play?" George suggested.

"Will you play with us too, Big George?" Little George pleaded.

George looked down at his nephew. "Tomorrow, maybe," he mustered, "Go with your friends."

Little George just stood there.

"Don't worry, Little George," he said. "I have things to do too. Leave me the book. I'll put it back on the shelf and cross your name off the sheet. We'll do some more math tomorrow."

They had left, and George began to search through the library. He recognized many names in the huge philosophy section. He finally located what he thought must be the primer: the Bible. He was stunned by how many different editions there were and pulled out the one nearest him: The New Oxford Annotated Bible. He signed the sheet, walked to an adult table, and put down the Book.

He sat, and without thinking put his elbows on the table, and held his head in his hands. He desperately wanted to run to the children, play with them: get lost in their world. He could not. The Dragon was coming. He was certain of it. And then there was his giant *I want*. He had dreaded facing them from the moment Junior had shown up that morning and taken Sarah from his arms.

His skyscraper had not crumbled, George saw in a flash. He had seen the Dragon arrive and destroy the City from the safety of his standing office. He was not stuck under the rubble. Was that why the dream had *moved* with him as he ran in the night? "You called the shots, George," Beth had said. He had helped the Dragon gain its grip on the world.

"How?" his mind howled. He had never intended to destroy people, enslave them. He wasn't Nero. He knew right from wrong. He had always played a clean game. He had always played by the rules.

A memory of his mother sitting alone exploded in his mind. They'd been at a party in one of the grand penthouses overlooking the City. Drinks were flowing, deals were being made, the musicians were playing in the corner. On his way back from the bathroom, he'd seen her, cowering in the shadows of the library. "What are you doing here?" he'd asked. "Why aren't you with the others on the terrace?"

She'd desperately wanted to be at that party, forcing him in that indirect way of hers to invite her. Someone – most likely she herself, he'd thought – must have said something that made her think that she didn't belong, and her reaction had proven the point. He had taken her hand, tucked it under his arm, and escorted her onto the enormous terrace.

He had made straight for Dieter and Irmgard, called for a waiter to bring a couple of drinks, and waved to Ralph, who didn't know German. 'Having' to translate for 'a bigshot' would make her feel superior, he knew, or at ease, which in her case was the same thing.

"Poor Mom," he sighed, the memory still making him cringe. How could she have expected to belong to his City world without following its rules? You don't let on that you care in the world of the "magic they." You don't show true need – or whine. You don't show yourself. You play the game, and win.

She had never understood the thing about worlds and their rules. You never "eat the last slice of pie" to belong to the gang at home. You "maximize profit," "control the market" to be a part of the City world. You "go to Mass" and "make donations" to belong to Church. It wasn't complicated.

Worlds are defined and distinguished by their own internal rules: they exist because of their internal rules.

Belonging to the worlds means following the rules. It is the rules that regulate interactions between people, define horizons, distinguish relevant from irrelevant information, differentiate between acceptable and non-acceptable behavior, set the parameters of conversations, and even their language.

Sam had never been able to communicate with any of the rest of them, his "family them" – which was really just his "siblings them" – because he had never really been "one of them." He always ate the last slice of pie.

His mother could never have belonged to his City world. She somehow wanted them to bow to *her* rules. Did she really expect them to go in and get her from the library?

It could become tricky if you belonged to many worlds. Different worlds have different rules, by definition. You have to keep them distinct in order to function, and for the worlds to exist. You cannot live by the rules of two different worlds at one and the same time. You cannot take a step holding a ball in basketball. You cannot dribble the ball in baseball. You have to fence off the worlds, or you end up always and never to have to dribble the ball. That is chaos. And chaos means that no set of rules is a real set of rules: that all rules are optional. That means no worlds. No baseball, no basketball.

To function you had to recognize the rules of the world to which you wanted to belong and play by them, locking all other rules and worlds into sealed compartments, which you opened when you wanted to enter them.

How could she *not* know these basic things? How could she insist on being "the mother" in his City world? George winced at the many times he had to bail her out of the messes that she had made and that had ended up hurting her so badly, making her so lonely.

The bell rang. It was time for the Angelus. George stood up, and heard others do so too. Someone in the library led the prayers. He responded. When they finished, he picked up the Bible and headed for the Common Room. He heard voices. They were all leaving. It would soon be dinner time.

20

He was slowly making his way through the tunnel.

Dinner had been a chance to "move" and to watch people "move." Little George had told Beth about "doing math with Big George. He promised to do math again tomorrow. And Tommy, Theresa, Daniel, and Adam will come too!" Beth had looked across the table at him and mouthed "Thank you." Mark, who had sat next to him again, had invited him to hunt. "Saw some wild hogs today. They'll be a problem come Spring. Some of the guys and I are getting a party together. Join us? Don't imagine you got much of a chance to hunt in the City." Rebecca had waved at him, Junior had nodded, and Little Sarah had given him a hug.

George had stayed as long as he reasonably could, just to soak it in – the voices, the children, that life that was so foreign and wondrous – and manned up. "See you tomorrow," he'd said to those who had not yet brought their children up to wash for bed, picked up the Bible, and made his way towards the tunnel.

He was alone. He didn't look in on the many rooms he passed. He'd seen the cheese, the weaving, the provisions.

Beth had really prepared, he told himself again. He had
no idea how much they consumed per day, or how much
they produced. Beth, he was sure, did, and had the numbers under control. They would not be visited by hazmats
any time soon. With that thought the dread of facing "it"
flooded his mind.

"Give it a name," he ordered, knowing that no one
would hear him: "The Dragon," he finally said, "Myself."

It was dark in the winery, George saw as he neared
the end of the tunnel. There was nothing but darkness
at the top of the stairs. He would soon have to turn off the
tunnel light. And then what? He couldn't make his way
through the fermenting room, reception room, back hall
without light. This wasn't his house.

He shook his head as he began to climb the stairs.
Why wouldn't there be a switch? Beth could not not have
thought of it.

Beth, he shook his head again, when he saw the fermenting room light switch next to the tunnel light one,
Beth. His wasn't envy. It was awe. Beth had seen what he
hadn't. That had never happened to George before.

The moon was shining through the windows in the
back hallway as he passed through, and in the kitchen. He
picked up the Violinist's note that was still on the dining
table and made his way to Paul's office. He had work to
do. The Dragon was coming. He would not let them be
poisoned. He would not do that again.

21

He was at Paul's desk. He had found paper and pencils. He put the Violinist's note in front of him, the Bible on the side. He was going to be systematic: define the problem and tackle it as he always had – study the data, find the key terms, see how they could fit together, identify the most likely ways in which they did, write them down, analyze his notes, write and rewrite them until something clicked and the underlying rules emerged.

He began with the problem, problems he realized as he wrote them in his fastidious hand:

a) the Dragon is coming;   b) I helped it;

c) I don't know how I helped it;   d) "Fiat mihi."

He could do nothing about a) or b). They were facts. He would have to face them at some point. It was not the time. That left c) and d). He would start with d): it was a key.

The data included 1) the Violinist's note and 2) the Gospel. He started with 1) the note:

Do not chase the dragon, let it come for you. It will come. It wants you. Its desire is for everyone. It does not often show itself. It prefers the dark. It slithers. You cannot defeat it alone.

Do not fear. Do not arm yourself.

Let in the light. Learn to see, to rejoice. The path is there for you to walk. You are not alone.

He read it several times, and homed in on three words: "alone," "arm," and "see." He wrote them down, adding "~" to the first two, making them "not alone" and "not arm."

Now for the Gospel. It had to be at the beginning of the Gospel, of one of the Gospels, he corrected himself. He flipped through Matthew, and Mark, and finally found it. It was Luke. Luke, then, chapter 1.

It was rife with crucial terms, more than he had encountered in any report that he had analyzed over the years. He would have to work hard and fast to identify them and see how they fit together. That didn't scare him. Everything could be tackled with method, focus, and obstinate work.

He wanted to do it in three days. The chapter had eighty lines, a nice, neat number. He would work on ten lines immediately, and then thirty-five lines on each of the next two days. He would get an earlier start.

George placed the Bible opened up on pp. 1240-1241 (the first pages of the Gospel) over to the left-hand side of the desk, put another piece of paper (tilted to the left) in the center of the desk, and began. He re-read the first paragraph carefully and wrote down three phrases in a first column: "things which have been accomplished," "eyewitnesses and ministers of the word," "that you may know the truth concerning the things of which you have been informed."

The first two were clearly parts of the puzzle: "Things which have been accomplished" overlapped with the let it be done. "Ministers of the word" had to do with the according to thy word – part of the equation. The third phrase was more complicated. He had included "That you may know the truth concerning the things" because it gave him hope. It made him think that the Gospel was a map – something that would show him a way out. He didn't know if (or how) it fit with the "Fiat mihi." He was also not sure what "eyewitnesses of the word" had to do with his puzzle, but knew that he would have to wait for the details. If he tried to define his terms too quickly, he would miss part of the picture. That was precisely what he could not afford.

He could feel his mind relax. He had begun, identified two possible pieces of the puzzle, and received confirmation that he had chosen the right book: "that you may know the truth concerning the things." His work for the night was not yet done. He needed to analyze six more lines.

He turned back to the text, reread the next paragraph, and began a second column where he wrote "righteous," "walking in all the commandments and ordinances of the Lord," and "barren." He did not know why "righteous" had jumped out at him, but "walking in the commandments and ordinances" clearly had to do with both doing and the word, and "righteous" was connected to it. "Barren," he thought, was related to "accomplished." It was the negation of accomplishable: a limit on the doing part.

He began a third column with the word "incense." There were many doings centered on incense, like burning and praying. There were also words involved in the actions that revolved around incense: in "prayers," mostly, but "custom" and "duty" – words that were also present in the lines – also involved words, somehow. He added "temple" to the list, and proceeded to look over all his words, fixing them in his mind.

George laid the yellow string on the appropriate page, carefully closed the Bible, stood up and stretched. He then opened the middle drawer of the desk and put his notes in it. The pencil he put back where he had found it: in the uppermost drawer on the left-hand side of the desk. It was time to sleep. He didn't know what to expect, said "Fiat mihi," and prepared for bed.

22

Friar Thomas was coming, or so the excited voices said at breakfast. He couldn't grasp what was so momentous about a man coming, but recognized that there was something different in the air: hope, joy. The children were running around chanting "Friar Thomas! Friar Thomas!" It was something like Christmas, the Christmases of his childhood.

He had had no dreams the night before, and had awakened with the words that he had written dancing in his head. He had grabbed his cold coffee, showered, dressed, picked up his notes and Bible, and headed for the Common Room.

It was just a matter of rules, he had seen. The Violinist's note was dotted with do nots and dos: a clear mark of rules. Luke too had rules: "commandments and ordinances of the Lord." Rules were something George understood. He knew rules. He just had to understand what specific ones they were.

George had smiled when he'd entered the Common Room, teeming as it was with excited people. He had headed straight for his table, smiled at Junior, Beth and their children, and sat, letting the words from his list dance in his head. He had taken some bacon and eggs from the platter, once it had gotten to him, and turned his focus inward. He did not want to lose his train of thought.

Little George came over to him as he got up to go to the library. "Will you take me to my confession?" he asked. "It's my first one, then I'll finally have communion. I want to be able to show myself." After a pause he whispered, "My mother and father have been arguing about giving the sacraments to Sarah. My father says she's too little. My mother says that we can't afford to wait. My father says not to worry: baptism is all she needs. My mother says we all need all the nourishment we can get. What do you say, Big George?"

"I'm on my way to the library to get some work done," George managed to say. "Shall we do some math this afternoon and talk about it then?" Beth's worry unnerved him. He smiled until Little George went off.

23

The library was empty. George found the table nearest the "talking corner," laid down his notes and Book, pulled out the chair, and sat. Thoughts were screaming at him, questions. Beth was taking measures to defend her people from the Dragon. How could she even know what she was up against? She had never seen the Screens' smoke, or heard their drivel about the "sacrifice" and the "common goo." She hadn't seen the tendrils, the crumbling skyscrapers. She lived in her world, a world of happy people fenced off from the other decaying worlds. How could she think that she could protect them?

George's eye was caught by the light refracting off the leather bindings of the "Classics." It suddenly hit him: electricity! Where did they get it? They had no generators. They had to be connected to the electric grid.

The enormity of it overwhelmed him. He had been all wrong! Beth hadn't fenced them off: shut them in a box. She worked with other worlds from within her Angelus world. That's how they had coffee! He knew they didn't produce it.

She knew. She knew about the Dragon. She knew about the decay. She had known all the while she had lived in her happy Angelus world.

Had he been told that he could live in more than one world at once, George would instantly have dismissed the claim. Different worlds have different rules: no one can simultaneously follow different sets of rules, play basketball and baseball at the same time. That was chaos. It would destroy basketball and baseball.

Beth did. He could not deny the evidence.

Questions about himself, his life, hovered in the corner of his mind, ready to burst and pull him into the dark place again. "Move," he said, "just move. The Dragon is coming," and forced himself to open Luke, read, and mentally annotate words and phrases. He had 35 lines to analyze.

He pulled out his notes, added "angel" to the third column, and began a fourth where he wrote "troubled/fear," "prayer heard," "son." He wrote without checking the text. He had memorized the key terms in the third and fourth paragraphs.

He reread the next three paragraphs to be sure that he remembered the terms, and wrote "how shall I know this?" "dumb," "not believe," in a fifth column. His sixth column had one phrase: "perceived that he had seen a vision." The seventh had two entries: "conceived," "reproach among men."

The eighth paragraph troubled him. He recognized the *Ave Maria*, but could not help wondering why it had been translated "Hail, O favored one, the Lord is with you" – which he thought clumsy, ugly, and doubtful. It also had a footnote that read, "Other ancient authorities add "Blessed are you among women." He quashed his irritation, picked his pencil back up and began an eighth column: "angel," "full of Grace," "considered in her mind," "troubled/fear." In the ninth column he wrote "how shall this be?" The tenth column had one word, "behold." In the eleventh he simply wrote, "Ecce ancilla Domini" – behold the handmaiden of the Lord – and "Fiat mihi" – let it be done to me. In the twelfth and last column he wrote "leaped," "voice," "blessed is she who believed." He sat back to analyze the words.

He took a blank sheet from his pile and began quickly to recopy his words in groups: "angel – troubled/fear," a combination that had appeared twice in the first 45 lines. "perceived – behold – informed," "walking in commandments – barren – reproach," "walking in commandments – "prayers heard" – "dumb," "blessed is she – dumb," "commandments – how shall I know this?"

There were levels and levels of combinations. "voice – dumb – perceived," "accomplished – conceived," "considered in her mind – behold," "angel – voice," "eyewitnesses – perceived," "prayer – walking in the commandments."

He filled pages and pages with notes, connected terms, made graphs. Questions were growing in his mind as he worked: Why – if Elizabeth was "righteous" – was her "barrenness" a "reproach among men"? Why – if Zechariah "walked in the commandments and ordinances of the Lord" – did he "not believe"? How did Mary see? "Blessed is she who believed." What did she see?

The bell rang. George stood up and heard another chair scrape the floor. It was the noon Angelus. "*Angelus Domini nuntiavit Mariae*" – the Angel of the Lord announced unto Mary, he heard a voice say, and responded, "*Et concepit de Spiritu Sancto*" – And she conceived of the Holy Spirit.

George left his notes on the table, as he had seen others do, and headed for the Common Room. "George?" he heard a voice call. It was Beth, who had a pencil holding up her hair. She looped her arm through his. "I'm starved," she said. "You? I hear we have fried chicken today! Rebecca's famous recipe."

They had poured in from all doors, grabbing their children, who were running. Silence had come over the room for a brief moment when Junior had called everyone to order for Grace, and then the wave-sound had formed anew. George just let it wash over him as he kept his mind focused on his terms.

He felt an elbow nudge him. It was Mark's. The chicken platter was being passed around at the table.

"Big George," a voice asked as he got up. It was Little George. "When are we doing math today? Before or after we play?"

"After," he heard himself say. He had to get back to his notes: the rules.

It was foreign to him, he realized as he sat at the table. It was not enough to "walk in the commandments." You had somehow also to have "things accomplished," things that were not consequences of following the commandments, "things" that could be perceived, witnessed, reacted to: "leaped."

Elizabeth had been "righteous" was "barren" and "reproached" for it. It made no sense. Why was she "reproached" for being "barren"? Having children was not a consequence of being "righteous." And then there was Zechariah, who had followed the rules and was punished for not believing.

Following the rules was not enough. You had to believe, so that something that did not follow from the rules could "be accomplished." Believe. Believe what? The rules?

Rules were not things you believed, he told himself. They simply defined a world to which you could belong if you knew and consented to the rules and applied them within the confines of the world they defined. Arithmetic was defined by "Zero is a natural number," "For every natural number x, x = x," and so forth. To belong to the world of arithmetic meant consenting to the rules and applying them within their world's confines.

You can't believe in rules. It had been his mantra since college, when he had understood in a flash that "Zero is a natural number" is inherently unintelligible. It entails a contradiction: that nothing is something classifiable. To believe "Zero is a number" is to believe what cannot be. No one can do that.

Not believing in rules had been the key to his success. It made him capable of moving with ease in each of his many worlds. Rules, he had convinced himself, were casual, random, inherently meaningless, like the color of one's socks. He could show that he did not care in the world of the "magic they" because he really didn't. It had been a game to him: an inherently meaningless game.

24

He felt more and more like Zechariah. "How shall I know this?" George asked and asked as he sat at his desk that night, his lamp the only dome of light in the winery.

He had read with Little George and his friends when they had shown up in the library, sounding out words with them. He had said the Angelus and dined with them all. He had rushed to Paul's office.

Like Zechariah he was afraid. The very fact that he was afraid troubled him. Why was he afraid? There was no angel standing before him, no grand message. He was alone.

Why, then, the fear?

Was it his own inability to understand? The fact that he, the person who had never not understood what he had decided that he needed to understand, was confused? Was he afraid that he would never understand? Or was it that he feared that there was *nothing* to understand? That all there is is a big, fat void: a chasm, space, emptiness?

He could not accompany Little George to his confession. He might be able to play in Beth's world, but he wouldn't toy with it. There were rules.

He put away his notes. No more Zechariah, puzzling over the world beyond the rules. He got ready for bed.

25

"She knows, you know," his mother said. "She knows you would have cut her financing, had you known. She knows your skyscraper did not crumble. They all know. She also knows that you don't believe her rules, the simpleton, with her sheep. Mrs. Smith was telling me the other day that she had a pied-à-terre in the City. It was not really hers, of course," she smirked. "Her son got a job and is living in a walkup studio apartment in Alphabet City. If she could only see this! Just look at that magnificent view!

"Who cares if you don't believe? if you don't understand the 'things to be accomplished?' You have a fine life without believing, without those other 'things.' I gave up long ago and look at this place: the Woolworth Pinnacle Penthouse!"

They were alone, sitting at the dining room table in his apartment. The leaves of the table had been pulled out. It was set. There was no food. He could see the skyline though the huge windows.

Who was coming? Where were the guests? Where was the food?

How could the skyscrapers still be standing? He had seen them crumble.

"You're making that face again, Georgie," his mother said, "that thinking face. Let it go. Leave it to her. There's no sense in struggling to believe in 'things accomplished.' Relax. Open your mouth," and reached out with a forkful of broccoli and tofu.

He woke in a sweat and threw himself out of bed. She knew. He knew Beth knew. What had she said? "You were a player . . . you determined the fates of economies and people."

And she had accepted him into her world: she let her children play with him. George couldn't breathe. The blackness was back.

Without thinking, he fell to his knees. "Please," he begged.

A violin broke through the stillness of the night. It was the Loure from Bach's Third Partita, the grave, pleading Loure. It washed over him. He couldn't hear it.

26

"You were a player," echoed in his head when he woke with a start the next morning. He jumped out of bed and headed for the refrigerator and his coffee. She knew.

George sipped the coffee, couldn't taste it, and went back to the office. "Move," he said, "just move." He put the coffee on the desk on a coaster and made for the shower. He needed to clear his head. The Dragon was coming. What could he do about it? He was just a businessman. What did he know about Zechariah, Elizabeth, "Fiat mihi"? His mother was right, for once: "Leave it to her."

The sun was skipping over the snow. The bare branches of the trees glistened. His steps cracked the ice covering the snow. He could hear it scrunch. He was making his way to the river. He needed to be alone. He needed the run.

"You made it!" he heard as he neared the bridge. "Didn't think you heard me last night." It was Mark, with Junior and a couple of other men. "Junior said you'd come. Your Winchester's with me," he called out.

George ran over to them. He vaguely remembered hearing Mark talk about the hunt and Winchester. "The wild hogs are in the woods over the bridge: two sows," Mark continued. "Let's split up in pairs."

The woods were still dark. He hadn't been in them since his teens. He had never heard of wild hogs roaming in these parts. They did a lot of damage, he knew. He and Mark were heading for the clearing, listening for sounds. The Winchester felt right in his hands.

A brown thing broke across the clearing. It was fast. George dropped to one knee, cocked, aimed, and fired, cocked again, and fired: once, twice. He waited. "Good shot," he heard. "That's one of them."

He stood back up and nodded, grateful that he had remembered his grandfather's advice and let out his breath as he dropped to his knee.

Mark was carrying one of the sows across his shoulders, Bill the other. Junior clapped him on the back. "Grandpa always said you were the best shot!" he said. "Next time we'll bring the boys." Nothing more was said as they made their way to the wing.

How did that happen? George's stunned mind asked. They'd waited, with his Winchester. "You cannot do it alone" blazed through him. The note, the Violinist's note.

27

They were in her quarters. George had said the Angelus, lunched, gone for his notes, and shown up at Beth's telling himself, *move, just move.*

"This is an impressive set of notes, George," Beth said, leafing through pages filled with terms, arrows, graphs, calculations of probability, modal reformulations, and all manner of refined analysis. "I haven't thought of half of these connections. Why have you come to me?"

He would have loved to jump right in and talk about the Dragon, the giant I want, the crumbling City, the Violinist's note, the rules. He didn't know how. "It's in my notes," he finally managed to say, and pointed.

Beth said nothing. She simply turned to his notes and began again to read.

George watched. She was completely immersed in thought. She emanated that same calm acceptance and trust that he felt in little Sarah.

The door swung open with a bang. Mike rushed in the room carrying a bird. "Mom," he said, "Mom – oh, hi Big George – I found it hopping on the ground by the willow" as he handed it to her. Beth took the bird in her hands.

"It's a robin, Mike," she smiled, and handed it back to him. "Give it some fruit. Raisins. Not too much food for it out there right now. The poor thing must be hungry." Mike nodded and hurried off to the kitchen, slamming the door with a bang as loud as his entrance's.

George watched Beth in awe as she took in her son's abrupt appearance. She did not flinch when the door slammed open, nor signal for her son to wait when he got to her side. She simply turned to him and focused on him. She could (and would) turn back to his notes, he knew, with the ease with which she had listened to her son and given him instructions.

"How do you do it?" he asked as the door slammed shut.

"Do what?" Beth asked.

"Switch worlds: focus on your son and his bird, while you are in the midst of reading my notes," George said. "You can live in two worlds at once."

Beth smiled, that splendid smile that pierced his fears. "They're not different worlds, George. Why would you think they are?"

"They follow different rules," he answered automatically. "Worlds are defined, constituted by rules. There are different sets of rules, so there are different worlds. Just as baseball has its rules and basketball its rules, and the worlds of baseball and basketball are different because they are constituted by different sets of rules, the world of robins has its rules, and Luke's world its own rules. We have separate sciences to study robins and Luke. Ornithology is not theology. It's basic."

"You got me there, George!" Beth laughed. "Ornithology is not theology. Birds are not God!"

George felt warmed by her quickness.

"But," Beth added after a pause and a wink, "yours is just a pretty piece of sophistry. If God created the universe, He must also have created the rules regulating the world of birds. Can the rules regulating the world of birds, then, really be distinct from the rules of God's world? And if they cannot be, and Luke deals with God's world, as you put it, can robins and Luke really belong to distinct worlds?"

"Touché," George said. She had cut through the worlds problem with astounding ease.

"Thank you," Beth replied with a grin and mocking a bow.

"You are of course right," he then added. "There are such things as *metarules*. I should have thought of that myself."

"No, George," Beth countered in a suddenly serious tone. "No. The real problem is *not* spelling out the logical entailments of Luke's world, as you call it. It is **not** formulating a set *metarules* that it might imply: *metarules* that could follow from it. The real problem is *accepting* Luke's world: knowing it, living in it. Luke's world is a tough pill to swallow, especially for us, Descartes's orphans, who think of everything as a game. We have to learn to accept reality."

The abrupt change in tone confused him. George sat very still, searching Beth's face for clues. "A game?" he asked. "Learn to accept reality?"

"Do you remember those old college games?" Beth finally said, "The ones where we were asked to enunciate something that we knew was necessarily true?"

George nodded, still scanning her face for a hint that might help him track her thoughts.

"Remember how those who asked would make us question the truthfulness of all our beliefs until we could find one that we knew with absolute certainty was true: a belief that could not not be true?"

He nodded.

"Remember, 'how do you know you're Beth?' or 'how do you know if your sensations are true?'"

"I remember very well," George responded, trying to understand what that game had to do with him, the rules, with worlds, with *games*, with *accepting reality*.

"You believe you're sitting here, really?" Beth giggled, "How do you know that you're not dreaming?"

"How do you know that there is no evil demon tricking you?" George added with a smile. "Tom, my roommate in college, went on and on for days pushing me to find a necessary truth."

"How did you deal with Tom, George?" Beth asked, suddenly serious again.

"I saw it was a game," he answered mechanically, "and that to win I had to use the rules against him."

"How?" Beth asked tilting her head. "How did you turn the rules against Tom?"

"After days of his pushing, I finally asked him if it is a necessary truth that there *is* a necessary truth," George said matter-of-factly.

"Slick, George," Beth responded with a nod of her own.

"Thanks," George said, and remembered Tom. "It trapped him," he continued, shaking his head. "My question trapped him. He became a professor someplace, and periodically sends me articles on necessity and modality. Poor Tom. He's still trying logically to prove that it is a necessary truth that there is a necessary truth, without begging the question. He's still stuck trying to beat me at that game."

"Ah, but you are too, George," Beth said quietly.

"What?" George asked. "I am also what?"

"Trapped," Beth whispered.

"Me?" George asked surprised. "I'm not stuck looking for necessary truths that don't beg the question."

"No," Beth confirmed. "You are not. You gave up on believing altogether."

She paused and caught his eyes. "In your case, George, the game turned everything into a meaningless set of arbitrary rules and the distinct worlds they 'constitute': the world of baseball, the world of robins, Luke's world. You defeated Tom because he believed in rules, silly ones, but he believed. He still believes. He just doesn't know how to articulate what he believes in, or why. You, on the other hand, are here so that I can help you believe again in something."

It felt like a punch. George let out his breath and lowered his eyes. "First round knockout," he said, wondering why he suddenly felt naked.

"No," Beth said, putting a hand on his arm. "I really meant it. What's tough about Luke's world is not deducing its logical entailments, but accepting it, knowing it, living in it. This is not a game, George. It's not about destroying your *modus ponens* with my *modus tollens*. It's not about seeing who has a quicker logical draw within the confines of an arbitrary world defined by a meaningless set of possible rules. **This is** about life, about reality. It is deadly serious. There is a real battle raging in the world. We are all of us in danger. It hungers for each of us."

"The Dragon," George responded, suddenly seeing something.

"The Dragon," Beth replied. "You were a player, George. You sat at the big table."

George lowered his head suddenly remembering his mother calling him "Georgie," and reaching out with a forkful of broccoli and tofu.

"Did you think I didn't know?" Beth asked.

George let his eyes trace the perimeter of the rhombus on the Karabakh rug under the coffee table.

Beth broke the silence. "There's a reason why you and your lot are called players, George. The world is a game to you: reality, all of it, a set of chess boards. Your problem, my friend, is that it really isn't a game, and you can no longer escape that fact. You want to stop playing. You just don't know how. You want to believe in something. You've been trying for days to muscle your way into belief from that tower from which you watch reality from the outside."

The memory of looking from his office at the rubble flooded George's mind. "I saw the destruction in a dream," he finally said, "the real battle raging: the Dragon destroying the skyscrapers. I watched. There were people stuck in the rubble."

"Were you unscathed in the dream?" Beth asked.

George lowered his head, the horror of it still bleeding into him.

"I'm not Joseph, or a dream reader," Beth said softly, "but you weren't really unscathed, were you?"

George looked up at Beth and shook his head. "Of course I was," he croaked. "I stood there at the window and watched, didn't I?" He closed his eyes and sucked in his breath as an image of his siblings sprawled on the couch flashed through his mind. It was not only in his dreams that people were being crushed by the Dragon. Heather, Eleonore, Helena, Brad, Sam were also being crushed.

"No, George," Beth's voice cut through his reeling mind. "You were not unscathed. You were, you *are* horror-struck: stuck under rubble of your own. It's written on your face."

He could hear the ticking of the clock and looked around for it. It was on the mantlepiece. She had a fireplace, he noticed for the first time. There was wood in it, ready to be lit. George smiled. It was the contingency plan, he saw, in case they were cut off from the gas line.

"George," he heard, "George?"

He looked over at Beth.

"What you don't know," she said, "is that you are really not in that tower looking at the destruction, at reality. You already are in reality, a reality you can't recognize."

He kept staring at Beth. The blackness was threatening at the corners of his mind.

She held his gaze and added in the softest voice, "I can't deduce that fact for you, George, as much as I would want to, so that you can follow my logic into reality. There is no mental bridge that can connect you to *what is*: no Archimedean point that can serve as a foundation from which you could deduce your way back into reality. You have to see it yourself: accept it."

"George," he heard her whisper, "you're a liability so long as you don't see."

George gazed at Beth's face, that calm, elegant, trusting face. "Do you want me to leave?" he managed to ask, knowing that it might be his lot, and ready to accept it.

"Good heavens, no," Beth laughed. "You won't intentionally hurt us, George. You love the kids. The problem is that the danger doesn't only originate in you. You have to open your eyes and see, so that it can't work through you."

Relief and confusion swept through him. He wanted to stay: to be with little Sarah, little George, to hunt, to search, to discuss, to understand. He could not, not if he put them in danger. There were rules.

But *how* could he be a liability if the danger did not come from him?

"It's those games, George," he heard Beth say. "They are at the heart of your confusion. They have trapped you: the question they're grounded on has trapped you. It's why you can't see."

"What question?" he asked.

"Zechariah's 'How shall I know this?'" Beth responded. "That's modern philosophy's question. It's the question we were asked to grapple with in college. It's the question that trapped Tom. It's the question that trapped you. It's a poisonous question that presupposes that we ought only to accept reality on our own terms. It's a false question. The simple fact is that reality *is* whether we accept it or not. *What is* does not come to be (or cease to be) because we do (or do not) accept it. *What is* does not bend to us. It is we who must bend to *what is*."

George closed his eyes and shook his head. It was too much, too fast.

"It's in your notes, George: 'walking in command-ments' – 'not believe' – 'dumb,' Beth insisted. "If I'm reading them right, you're asking why Zechariah was held accountable for asking for proof."

George felt his mind focus: the notes, Luke, Zechariah. "Yes," he said, "Zechariah! 'walking in commandments' – 'not believe' – 'dumb.' Why was he struck dumb? Belief isn't a necessary consequence of 'walking in the commandments.' It's in the text. Luke says that Zechariah was 'righteous' and he didn't believe. So why was he punished for not believing? He was struck dumb for something that did not make him unrighteous."

"Ah," Beth rejoined, "But the text does not say that he was 'righteous' *while* he didn't believe. It couldn't, George. The first Commandment is 'I am the Lord your God,' and the second 'Thou shalt not take the name of the Lord in vain.' Questioning God's messenger is both not treating God as Lord, and taking His name in vain."

"Why, then," George fired back, why does Luke say Zechariah was 'righteous?'"

"Because Zechariah was 'righteous' *until* the angel appeared. It was doubting the angel that was 'unrighteous.' He was punished for that doubt. Believing God is a necessary part of 'righteousness.'"

"Why?"

"What is 'unrighteous' about asking, 'How shall I know this?' Is that the question?" Beth asked.

"Yes," George said.

"Zechariah had every reason to believe the angel," Beth responded quietly. "He was a priest, well-versed in the prophets, who had foretold exactly what he was hearing;

he was in the temple, at the right-hand side of the altar; he was praying. He was afraid, of course: the appearance of an angel must be startling. But once it passed, Zechariah should – by all rational standards – simply have rejoiced at being visited by the messenger of God, at the message. He didn't. He simply didn't believe the angel. He asked, 'How shall I know this?'"

"Why is that unreasonable to ask?" George pushed.

"In order to ask it," Beth replied, "Zechariah has to have assumed that the angel was not trustworthy, that the prophets weren't trustworthy, that the temple was not really holy, that he could only really trust himself: accept only what he himself clearly and distinctly under-stood to be true, accept what is on his own terms.

"The only way to get to Zechariah's question, in other words, is to reject reality, history, the sacred. It's tragic when priests do that: it's a betrayal of their vows, their role. But it's not just priests who do. We can all reject real-ity, what is around us, what we ourselves are, and accept only what we clearly and distinctly understand to be true: decide to accept reality only on our terms. That's pride at its worst and most destructive."

What is blazed through George's mind. "It's wrong," he asked tentatively, "because it requires a rejection of *what is?*"

Beth smiled, that beautiful smile that warmed him. "Yes!" she beamed. "But not just the rejection of *what is* around us. It also requires a rejection of what we ourselves are: of my *what is*, of the *what is* that is you. We're a *part* of reality, George, not the *whole* of it. Our job is to interact with *what is*. That interaction is crucial to each of us, to our growth. We cannot interact with reality if we want to start from what we know is clearly and distinctly true. We are simply not built immediately to be able to understand what is clearly and distinctly true and proceed from there.

"Children cannot only accept what they already understand is true," she continued, "if they are going to learn anything. They first have to trust their parents (and teachers). Their minds must grow first. What can a 3-month-old understand about the world, or about the trustworthiness of what he is told about the world? How about a 12-year-old? So are they supposed not to trust what they see, what they are told? Put the flow of information on hold until they are in a position to determine its veracity? How could they even get into that position if they put the flow on hold? How could their minds grow? How could they learn?

"I just told Mike that he was holding a robin, and that he should feed it raisins. Mike didn't assume I was lying and ask for proof. He didn't assume that the bird was a hallucination. He trusts his perceptions. He trusts the world. He trusts me. I have tried to be worthy of that trust. Without that trust he can't learn, he can't come to understand if and why what I am teaching is true.

"The same thing holds for us. We're not all that different from children, really. A bit farther down the road, I hope, but we're still learning. Our minds, I pray, are still growing, developing the capacity to take in the world, to know it."

The bell rang for the Angelus. They both stood, and George intoned, "Angelus Domini nuntiavit Mariae" – the Angel of the Lord declared unto Mary – and Beth responded, "Et concepit de Spiritu Sancto" – and she conceived of the Holy Spirit.

"Sorry, for the rant, George," Beth said when they had finished reciting the Angelus. "I get caught up in it because the angel who punished Zechariah for his pride didn't mete out the same punishment to Descartes, or those who followed him and have written drivel for centuries and ruined the lives of many. It breaks my heart to think of the children who are told that they already know what they are, who they are, that they don't have to listen to their parents. We are coming apart as a society, and at the seams, because of them."

It was almost dinner time. George reached for his notes. Beth looked up at him from her seat with eyes filled with a tenderness that he had never known. "It's all much simpler and more beautiful than you think, George," she said. "There is only one universe by definition, and all things and actions in it are part of a magnificent tapestry that is being woven with and through them. We were each of us created with love. Seeing it starts by accepting what is around you, before you. You just have to learn to see."

George absorbed the tenderness.

28

"My Daddy says Big George works with the Dragon," a tiny voice – Adam's? – said. "He says Big George should leave. That the Dragon will come here if Big George is here." "Nah-uh," a girl's voice – Teresa's? – responded. "Big George is nice and my Daddy says we are safe here."

George was returning to the winery with his notes. He had a half-hour till dinner. He needed to reflect. The children didn't know that he could hear them. There must have been ten of them telling each other what their respective parents had said about him. From the sound of things, a fight was about to break out.

"You're wrong!" – it was Little George – "Big George isn't the Dragon. He can't fly." "My Daddy said he flew to China and that's where the Dragon is from." The voice was another boy's – Tommy's. "How could he fly if he isn't the Dragon?"

"That's just stupid." It was Little George. "George is the Dragon," a little voice said, "George is the Dragon."

"Ow! You kicked me!" That was Tommy's voice.

A child began to shriek. The shriek was joined by sobs, and quickly by the voices of worried parents who had arrived at the scene. "Stop that!" Big George could hear them say. "But he started it." "What's going on here?" The last voice was Junior's.

George turned and started to walk towards the stairs to the cellar. He could hear shouting.

29

The weight of the words seemed to grow with every stair. "George is the Dragon." A memory flashed through George's mind: "Quality is an expense," he heard a young himself say, "cutting expenses is maximizing profits. Quality is expendable. Quantity can replace quality." He'd gotten the promotion. Many local industries had closed. Profits had grown exponentially. Quantity, he discovered, is profitable in itself.

Mom was right. He would have cut their financing without a care in the world.

"I was just following the rules," he wanted to say. He couldn't. It was a lie. He'd wanted to belong, to be "a part of it," to show them. He'd come to articulate the rules himself.

"George is the Dragon," he said out-loud when he got to the last step.

His grandfather had tried to warn him that Christmas when they had spent the night in the winery far from his family. "Careful George," he had said over a glass of Old Vine Zinfandel, "you cannot touch the land from the City, watch the grapes grow and ripen. You don't have to bend your back or knee in an office to tend the roots of a vine. You won't see what you love, or how to protect it. Careful, or you'll lose sight of what is." His grandmother had come in with a pecan pie. "He's a good boy, Grandpa," she'd said. "Let him spread his wings." "You can't get anything real done out of anger," his grandfather had answered. "I could never forget," George had promised. "You and Grandma, the house. My clippers are here, and my Winchester. I'll be back, you'll see, and we'll go on another hunt, and harvest the grapes." He'd meant it.

He couldn't undo it. His grandfather died during one of his trips to the Far East. They'd never gone on another hunt. The market had centralized, "globalized." He had gotten rich: rich beyond belief. The people had been seduced by him and his I want. His skyscraper had not crumbled: they had been caught in the rubble. "If hell is paved with good intentions," he snarked, "Mine were golden."

Of course they thought he was the Dragon. He had left nothing but slaves and destruction in his wake. His own siblings had turned into animals.

The lights went off in the tunnel. It was pitch black. He stopped. He must be halfway through, he thought. "Hello?" he called. "Hello?" No door opened. No light. "Hello?" Why should they help him?

"And you think they're right not to serve you?" he heard a voice echo in the tunnel. "Don't you see them, those frightened sheep fighting each other? They must bend to one of the designers of the great game."

"Who are you?" George asked.

In rapid succession, George suddenly saw Heather staring at the ceiling, Helena at her hands, Brad saying

"It's not my fault," Sam with his head on his mother's lap, the skyscrapers crumbling, his mother reaching out with a fork with broccoli and tofu, the parents in Beth's wing fighting, their twisted faces shouting, skeletons of persons wearing rags huddled beneath the walls of a Middle Eastern city, skeletons of persons wearing striped uniforms standing in line for a bowl of soup, rows and rows of children with swollen bellies in a frozen world, prisoners huddled in camps, their guards whipping them, children reaching for a piece of bread that some sadistic person in a suit was holding out of in front of them.

"I can reach where I want, when I want," the voice said. "Look, just look at them, at the pitiful image and likeness: the stewards of creation. I can make them hate each other, kill each other, hate themselves, kill themselves. The world is mine. How can they be the stewards? They're giving me their children."

"It's your plan?" George asked. "It's all *your* plan?"

"Bow to me," the voice said.

"Bow?" George asked surprised.

"I spared your skyscraper," the voice said.

"You're the Dragon?" George asked. "You?"

"Bow to me," the voice said.

"There's a real Dragon!" George shouted. "It's not just us! not just me!"

"Bow to me and rule!" the voice commanded.

"Bow and rule? Rule? You work through us?" George asked stunned by the thought. "You work through us whether we know it or not? It was your plan?"

"I can reach where I want, when I want," the voice said.

"I want!" George said, and saw the giant I want, the giant I want that had been Nero's, that was his, that was the "magic they's." The giant I want that twists what is: the I want that rejects what is to rebuild what is.

Fiat mihi then blazed in his mind: "conceived," "son," "voice," "leaped for joy," "blessed is She who believed." "There is what is!" he cried. "It is! It is 'accomplished through us' with us. It starts with a 'Yes' to what is. Mary said 'Yes' to what is. 'Let it be accomplished.' Zechariah didn't trust what is."

"Worship me!" the voice commanded. "The order is what I want."

There were two teams working through what is, George saw: the "yes" team and the "no" team, the "what is" team, and the "what I want" team. He had played for the wrong one.

"NO!" George shouted. "I let you twist what is through me. Twist me if you must, whoever you are. You seem to need 'sacrificial victims.' God knows I deserve it. Just leave them, them all, leave what is alone."

The lights came back on. It was gone.
He started to walk again.

He could see the end of the tunnel and the stairs that led to the winery. There was light coming from the fermenting room. He could hear the violin. It was the

Preludio of Bach's Third Partita. He began to run, and took the stairs three at a time.

Light was emanating from the kitchen. He could smell the roast lamb, the rosemary.

"Two plates?" he asked, when he got to the kitchen and headed towards the cabinet. "Yes," he heard, and his heart leapt.

30

He woke, jumped out of bed, and went to the window.

The tapestry of lights twinkling on the deep greyish-bluish dancing surface of the river was back, as were the deeper blue swaths where the currents pushed under the surface. He watched as the dance of the shimmering lights began to engulf the swaths, pulling them into their laughter.

"Yes," he heard and that joyous laugh. "It will be made anew, and rejoice. Breakfast is ready!"

3I

Junior, Beth, Gabe, Mike, Anne, Cece, little George, little Sarah, Tommie, Adam, Teresa, Mark, Rebecca, waved at them. He and the Violinist, whom they knew as Friar Thomas, would go to the big house. Beth had given them food for the house, provisions from her wing. Little Sarah had given him a kiss for them, Little George a note, Junior a clap on the back. Mark held on to the Winchester. They would be back.

George gazed at the path between the vineyards as they walked. He finally recognized that yearning, that breathtaking yearning that he had felt when they used to drive through those long tunnels on the highway what felt like an eternity ago: the certainty that there was something beyond, and that he was making for it.

ABOUT THE AUTHOR

Siobhan Nash-Marshall is a Professor of Philosophy and the Mary T. Clark Chair of Christian Philosophy at Manhattanville College in New York. A prolific author, her latest publications include *The Sins of the Fathers: Turkish Denialism and the Armenian Genocide* (2018), that has been translated into Italian and Armenian. She publishes regularly in the *Imaginative Conservative*, and elsewhere. Prof. Nash-Marshall enjoys lecturing and does so often, both at home and abroad, where she is often invited. She loves life, music, novels, and challenges. Her favorite animal is the human being. She set up a non-for-profit to protect that vilified species.

Also by Siobhan Nash-Marshall

Joan of Arc. A Spiritual Biography
ISBN 9780824599058

What It Takes to Be Free.
Religion and the Roots of Democracy
ISBN 9780824519940

Participation and the Good.
A Study in Boethian Metaphysics
ISBN 9780824518523

The Sins of the Fathers.
Turkish Denialism and the Armenian Genocide
ISBN 9780824523787